To JAKE
(D)IANA'S YOUNG
NEIGHBOUR

LOTSALOVE
TERRY x

Terry Lambert

Terry Tarbox worked for many years in the retail furniture trade, but has also been a postman, a milkman, an ice-cream seller and manager of a pet cemetery (a job he soon decided was not for him). Now retired, his hobbies are gardening, reading and writing. He loves working on his allotment, and that is where he thinks up most of his stories. He blames *Spike Milligan*, *The Goon Show* and *Monty Python's Flying Circus* for the level of humour in his tall tales. Having struggled with depression for many years, he cites story-writing and the strong support of his friends and family as the things which have kept him on track. He lives in Lowestoft, Suffolk.

THE WILLIGREWS
2

Terry Tarbox

Illustrations by WW Design
ww.design@btinternet.com
01825 768518

ISBN 13: 978-1506082578

ISBN-10: 150682572

DEDICATION

This book is dedicated to Sylvie & Bill Jagger of Blyth Valley Community Radio for their continued support and encouragement

CONTENTS

**All illustrations in this book are by
Wendy Wheatley**

Hello, again, I was just thinking about you! How has life been treating you, since we last spoke? Well, I hope.

I expect you have been wondering what has been happening with the Willigrews, or perhaps you haven't. Well, if you have a few minutes I'll tell you anyway.

THE WILLIGREWS

THE WILLIGREWS AND HESEP

One morning, as the Willigrews were going about their usual business of weeding the chickweed beds and being silly in a general way, Krowfin turned to Longstint and asked, 'Did you see some movement in the bushes over there just then?'

Longstint looked toward where Krowfin was pointing and replied, 'No, what do you think it was?'

'I'm not sure, but it was white and was moving rather quickly,' said Krowfin, still peering into the bushes.

Longstint didn't seem too concerned and said it was probably one of those quick moving white things that we all see from time to time, and carried on weeding.

'Quick, look up, there it is again,' cried Krowfin, pointing once more.

'Oh, yes, I see it now, sort of white and a bit fluffy. I wonder what that can be?' asked Longstint. 'Shall we go and take a look, might be interesting?'

The two little friends strolled over to the edge of the chickweed beds, being a bit careful, not wanting to frighten whatever it was, away.

They didn't have to worry because the creature did not seem at all scared and greeted them with a cheery wave.

It looked a bit like a sheep, with a woolly coat, and a little black nose. It had four legs in all, one in each corner.

'Hello there, my name is Hesep, half sheep, half sheep, what is yours?' it said.

The Willigrews introduced themselves and welcomed Hesep to their village.

Longstint then asked Hesep, 'What brings you to this neck of the woods, friend; we haven't seen you around before?'

Before Hesep could answer, Krowfin

interrupted and asked, 'I didn't know woods had necks, do they have arms and legs as well?'

The other two didn't answer, and Hesep said, 'Well, to tell you the truth, and it embarrasses me to say this, but I think I may be lost. I went on my usual weekly hunting trip, which I do every day, this morning and seem to have lost track of time.'

'Well, perhaps if you can tell us where you live, we may be able to help you find your way home,' said Krowfin, helpfully.

'I live in a bucket,' explained Hesep, ignoring the surprised looks on the faces of the Willigrews.

'In a bucket?' asked Longstint, his eyes wide open and his nose pointing forward (his ears stayed where they were). 'Isn't that a bit uncomfortable, how do you get to sleep at night?'

'Oh, it's easy; I make myself comfortable by wrapping my legs around my body and turning myself inside-out; it is then very comfortable. Well, to tell the truth, I have to do this so that I am able to fit inside the bucket,' Hesep explained.

'Interesting,' remarked Longstint, 'but

what were you hunting for?'

'Puddles,' replied Hesep, 'lovely puddles. You see what with there having been very little rain lately; puddles are becoming a bit scarce where I live.'

Noticing that the Willigrews were looking a bit curious Hesep proceeded to explain. 'I get all my nourishment from puddles; I have to drink puddle water on a regular basis to keep well. I know puddle water would not be healthy to Willigrews and other tribes but to me, it is vital for my well-being.'

'Right,' said Krowfin, 'shall we get you home now? If you could tell us where you live we will accompany you.'

So off the little trio went, in the direction that Hesep had come from. While they were walking along Longstint asked their new friend what tribe she came from and what it was called.

'My tribe is called the Heseps,' replied Hesep.

'So you are Hesep Hesep,' said Longstint, looking a touch baffled.

'Exactly,' replied Hesep, with a little laugh, 'we are all called Hesep Hesep.'

'Well that's a bit strange,' commented

Krowfin. 'How do you know who is whom, or is that whom is who or perhaps who is who, I don't think it's whom is whom?'

Disregarding Krowfin's waffling Hesep said, 'We say the names in a different tone of voice. I will explain if I may. When my friends address me, they say my name in a normal voice, whereas when they speak to my best friend Hesep they say it in a high-pitched voice. We mostly live alone in our buckets, but do meet up every second Wednesday on the third Friday in every fourth month.'

The three little friends carried on until they came upon a fork in the path, but left the fork for someone who had lost a fork and might come looking for it.

'Can you remember which direction you came to this fork from Hesep?' asked Longstint.

However, Hesep could not remember, she said that all the paths look the same and she was concentrating on looking for puddles at the time.

Longstint decided to toss a leaf to help them decide. The leaf did a twisty turny journey in the air and landed on the side that would send them left, so off they went, hoping it was the right path (although it was the left path).

As they poodled along, to the Willigrews delight, Hesep started singing a little song. (The Willigrews loved little songs. They loved big songs as well, even medium songs). The little song went something like this:

I am a Hesep,
I sing a song as I walk along,
Not a Jessop,
It makes me happy so it can't be wrong.
Yes, I'm a Hesep.

I look for puddles,
And if I find one I take a sip,
From lovely puddles,
They make me happy so I hop and skip.
Around the puddle.

Sing like the Heseps sing,
Walk like the Heseps walk,
Talk like the Heseps talk,
All the livelong day.

Hesep repeated the song, and of course, the Willigrews joined in, hopping and skipping along the path. They were all having a lovely time until, suddenly, Longstint stopped and looked over to his left into the bushes.

He pointed to a particular spot and the others looked. What they saw was a pair of large black eyes peering over the top of a small bush. As the creature started to stand up, the black eyes were followed by a large fat body; the large fat body was covered in stiff spiky whiskers.

The Willigrews stood still, frozen with terror, but they were sparked into action when Hesep shouted, 'Run for your lives it's a Whiskerdon.'

Longstint and Krowfin, needing no further

urging, did exactly as Hesep had told them, and started running away from the large scary Whiskerdon as fast as their little Willigrew legs would take them.

They ran as fast and as far as they could, until Hesep spotted a hole in the bottom of a dead tree. They ducked inside, hoping that the monster was too large to follow them.

They kept quiet and listened, and then they heard a loud snuffling sound. Longstint peeked out of the tree trunk and there it was, looking around and sniffing the air.

It was huge, it had a large bulbous head with two eyes that stuck out on stalks, its body, as I said, was covered in the most horrible sharp whiskers and its feet were large and knobbly. It gave out a loud deep-throated roar and streams of snot dripped from its flat leathery nose.

Hesep spoke, with a quiver in her voice, 'If that thing catches us we are dead; it will eat us all in one mouthful!'

'How come we haven't seen one before?' asked Krowfin. 'We would have noticed something that big and fearsome.'

'I have seen one from a distance,' said Hesep, 'but it is unusual to see one this far south. I heard that one attacked the Mixdames' village further north and ate most of the inhabitants.'

'How terrible' exclaimed Longstint, 'those poor creatures. I hope it doesn't find Willigrew.

They watched and waited, hoping against hope that the monster wouldn't spot them. Eventually it scratched its head, looked about once again and headed off.

'Thank goodness,' said a relieved Hesep, 'it's going away; we can carry on in a minute or two. Was that Whiskerdon big, or was it big. I tell you what, it was bigger than big, even bigger than very big, it was mahoosive!'

'Wait a minute though,' gasped Krowfin, 'look where it's heading, straight for our village!'

'Oh no,' cried Longstint, 'we must stop it.'

Then, to the Willigrews amazement, Hesep ran after the Whiskerdon and started shouting at it, 'Oy, big ugly thing, you don't frighten us, you'll never catch us, you are too fat and slow and anyway you need a shave.'

The Whiskerdon turned immediately and faced little Hesep. Very scared, but very brave Hesep waved the monster on, 'Come on then, if you think you're hard enough,' she shouted, challenging it to fight.

The Whiskerdon advanced and Hesep retreated, running away with the two Willigrews close behind her. Although the monster was very big, it was very quick and pursued the little trio relentlessly.

'I think you've upset it Hesep, it looks a bit miffed,' said Longstint breathlessly.

Hesep suggested they split up to confuse their pursuer, so Longstint went left, Krowfin went right and Hesep went straight ahead. It followed Hesep, which allowed the other two to slow down a little.

They watched as Hesep dodged and weaved about, but the Whiskerdon was getting closer with every stride. The Willigrews followed at a safe distance and were becoming very worried that the Whiskerdon would catch Hesep.

'Oh no,' cried Longstint, 'they are heading straight for the crumbly cliffs; Hesep will be trapped!'

Just as they feared, Hesep ran blindly, it seemed, toward the cliffs. The Willigrews shouted for her to stop and to distract the Whiskerdon. Too late, there was no stopping Hesep, and the Willigrews held their breath as she headed straight for disaster.

Longstint gasped as Hesep, not stopping for even a second went headlong over the edge, disappearing into the void.

The Whiskerdon followed right to the edge and stopped just in time. However, it lost its balance and tried desperately not to fall. It leaned back trying to avoid the drop, and then, waving its arms about, toppled forward and, despite its efforts, fell head first over the cliff edge.

Still angry, the monster screamed as it hurtled toward the rocks below, where it smashed into the ground with a very loud splat.

Neither Longstint nor Krowfin wanted to

look over the cliff, not wanting to see poor Hesep squashed up.

So, they walked sadly away toward Willigrew and home.

Krowfin said, tearfully, 'So sad to lose such a brave and lovely friend.'

'Yes,' agreed Longstint, 'she saved our lives and we can never thank her.'

However, they had not gone more than a few yards when they thought they heard something.

'I just heard something,' said Longstint (see, I told you they did).

'So did I, and I think it was Hesep's voice,' cried Krowfin, excitedly.

Sure enough, Hesep was shouting, 'Help, help, I am down here.'

The two little Willigrews ran over to the edge of the cliff to see Hesep balanced on a very narrow ledge.

'Hang on Hesep,' called Longstint, 'we will help you, but keep very still.'

'I've got an idea, find some ivy, and then we can pull Hesep up.'

Krowfin dashed off to find the ivy while Longstint tried to reassure Hesep by talking to her.

Krowfin soon came back with some long pieces of ivy and tied one end around his waist. Longstint, not giving a thought to his own safety grabbed the loose end and started to abseil down to Hesep.

He couldn't help noticing the dead Whiskerdon lying on the rocks below and felt a bit sad.

'OK, Hesep, I am going to get you out of here,' said Longstint, who then tied the ivy around her waist. 'I don't think Krowfin will be able to pull you up on his own, so I will climb back up to help him.'

Longstint climbed, hand over hand, back up the ivy and was soon standing next to Krowfin. Between them, they started to haul their friend to safety.

It was hard work, because Hesep was quite heavy, but eventually she was safely back with the Willigrews.

'Thank you both, very much, you have saved my life,' said a relieved Hesep.

'Don't mention it,' said Longstint, patting Hesep on the head, 'it's the least we could do, considering how brave you were, now let's get you back to Willigrew.'

Hesep was limping a little and had quite a

few scratches on her legs, so the Willigrews supported her on the journey back home.

When they were nearly there, it started to rain quite heavily, which pleased Hesep, because there would now be puddles to drink.

On arrival back at the village, Hesep was introduced to everyone and then taken to Doc Dickery, who dressed her wounds (in a nice little pink frock with red bows), and told her to rest for a few days.

Yill, who had quite taken to Hesep, went on a scouting mission to find a puddle, and as it had been raining, there were quite a few.

Hesep gratefully slurped her way through a whole puddle and thanked Yill.

As it was now getting late, Bronglay offered Hesep a bed for the night, but Longstint explained about her sleeping in a bucket.

Krowfin found what he thought would be a suitable one and put it outside in front of the Meeting Hall.

The Willigrews, being rather inquisitive creatures, gathered around to see Hesep prepare for bed.

She stood in the bucket on her hind legs wrapped both front legs around her fleecy body and to the amazement of all, turned herself inside out.

She then slid down inside the bucket, wished everyone goodnight and went to sleep.

'It's funny really,' remarked Longstint, 'we usually turn in for the night, but Hesep turns inside-out for the night.'

Everyone laughed and all the Willigrews went home to bed.

The End

THE WILLIGREWS AND THE GHOST THAT MAY HAVE LIKED PILCHARDS

One sunny day our little friends were going about their usual business of growing chickweed and being very silly when they were disturbed by Krowfin running across the field shouting at the top of his voice, and he had a really tall voice, 'Someone's nicked me pilchards!'

The others stared at Krowfin as he ran around in medium sized circles waving his arms in the air and shouting, 'My pilchards have gone; someone's nicked me pilchards!'

'Where will I find a better source of Omega 3?' he asked, not expecting a reply.

Nobody replied (see, he was right) but they all stood staring in amazement at Krowfin whose little green face was rapidly turning a shade of little deep red.

Bronglay put his arm around Krowfin and tried to reassure him 'Don't take on so, Krowfers old chap. It's not the end of the world as we know it.'

'All this fuss about a little tin of pilchards,' said Dora, raising an eyebrow (it was Rewsin's eyebrow).

Krowfin was a bit miffed at this and complained. 'It wasn't just one tin. I had ten tins in the cupboard and eleven of them have disappeared.'

Krowfin explained that he noticed the pilchards were missing when he went to the cupboard to get some out for breakfast. He thought it must have happened while he was asleep.

'Well,' said Bronglay, 'we know that they were not stolen by a Willigrew, so who could have taken them?'

Longstint thought it might be a gang of ruthless tinned fish thieves that, at any moment, could strike again without warning.

The others thought this a bit far-fetched and dramatic but Longstint was not convinced.

'Mark my words,' he said, 'by tomorrow there won't be a pilchard to be found in the whole of Willigrew!'

'In fact,' he continued, 'Willigrew will be a pilchard-free zone, and we'll all become ill through a serious lack of Omega 3.'

'Let's all have a nice cup of chickweed tea and try to think of a plan to sort this problem out,' suggested Bronglay.

The others agreed so they all sat down on

the ground and started to think.

However, Bronglay (who else) finally came up with an idea.

He explained, 'OK my little green gooseberries, I would like you to gather up all the pilchards in the village and take them to the Meeting Hall. We will put them there and place a guard over them for the night and see what happens.'

Longstint was first to volunteer to be one of the guards followed by Zamborina.

The Willigrews then wandered off in different directions to bring the pilchards from their homes.

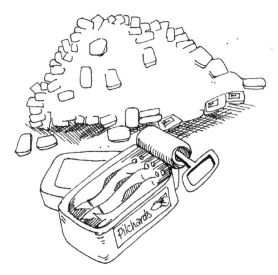

After about half an hour, all the pilchards

were stacked in a neat pile in one corner by the stage.

The whole tribe gathered in the hall, which prompted one to remark, 'We're packed in like sardines!'

This confused Krowfin and he said 'Pilchards? Sardines? I'm confused' (see I told you he was).

Bronglay hopped up onto the stage. He just felt like hopping, well don't you sometimes just feel like hopping. I know I do.

'OK everyone,' he began, 'settle down now. I suggest you all go home to bed and let the guards do their jobs, and we'll find out what happens tomorrow.'

He then asked them all to meet at eight o'clock the following morning to find out what happened.

They all wandered off again, saying things like 'goodnight and see you in the morning,' etc., not that anyone actually said, etc., well you know what I mean, I hope.

Longstint settled down next to Zamborina to wait for something to happen to the pilchards. They sat cross-legged on the floor at the end of the hall opposite the stage and tried to stay alert.

They had brought a flask of chickweed tea and some Jangleberry cake to keep them going. Then they watched the pile of tinned pilchards very carefully.

Longstint turned to Zamborina and asked, 'Like some tea?'

'Yes please,' replied Zamborina, holding out her cup.

The two then sat drinking the tea and started talking about the pilchard mystery.

'I wonder what it's all about,' said Zamborina, scratching her fingernails but still keeping an eye on the pile of pilchard tins for any sign of activity.

'Who knows?' replied Longstint. 'Perhaps it's something to do with pilchards in general, perhaps they all disappear eventually. Perhaps it's just the way of things with pilchards, and it may just be in their nature to disappear.'

'It might be in the genes,' said Zamborina.

For a moment, the two Willigrews pictured a pilchard wearing jeans and both smiled, but said nothing.

'One thing I do know,' said Zamborina.

'What's that,' asked Longstint, quizzically.

'Things are more like they are now than

they have ever been before,' she replied, looking a bit confused.

Longstint didn't comment.

At first, nothing happened, and Longstint and Zamborina started to nod off. Suddenly, however, Longstint thought he saw something move, it was a tin of pilchards.

It seemed to rise into the air and float toward the door. He couldn't believe his eyes (although his eyes had always been truthful before).

After waking Zamborina. Longstint said to the tin, in a serious voice, 'Get back with the other tins please.'

Nevertheless, the tin couldn't have been listening (in my experience tins never listen) and continued floating toward the door.

'Did you hear what I said?' asked Longstint, but the tin didn't reply. I suppose that was because tins don't normally have ears.

Longstint felt a shiver run down his spine as he realised that a ghost was stealing the tin of pilchards!

By the way, the shiver eventually ran back up his spine, sat on his shoulder, curled up and went to sleep.

Zamborina followed Longstint and, as our little heroes approached the floating tin, it disappeared through the closed door.

'Ooer!' exclaimed Longstint, 'I think I might be a bit frightened.'

Zamborina reassured Longstint by holding his hand.

After a few minutes, another tin began to float upwards.

When Longstint saw this, he rushed over and grasped the tin in his hand.

As soon as he touched it, a shape appeared from thin air, it was a ghost!

I expect you would like to know what the ghost looked like; well all right, I'll tell you then.

This was one weird spirit, tall and skinny with a centre parting in his hair!

It was difficult for Longstint to get a good look because it kept fading away and becoming clear again. Then, to his surprise, the ghost let out a loud howling sound.

'Owoooooh!' it went.

'What was all that about?' said Longstint. 'It wasn't very scary.'

'Wasn't it?' replied the ghost looking a bit embarrassed.

'Well, you see, I haven't been ghosting for very long, and I'm still taking ghostly wailing lessons. I've almost got the disappearing bit right but the wailing is taking a bit longer, and as for GCSE Poltergeisting Stage 2, I'm total rubbish.'

'I can manage to do them one at a time, but I'm not very good at multitasking.'

'They do need some work,' remarked Longstint. 'Perhaps you should switch to a side parting.'

'I've tried that, but it just naturally goes to the centre,' said the ghost.

'More to the point, why are you stealing our pilchards?' asked Longstint.

'Well,' the ghost replied, 'when I was alive I just loved pilchards, couldn't get enough of them, but now I'm a ghost I don't need to eat to stay alive because I'm not alive if you see what I mean. Now I'm not sure whether I like them or not. Anyway this is all part of my ghost exam.'

The ghost then explained that the first task in the exam offered three choices.

1. Steal a quantity of canned fish, which is rich in essential Omega 3 oils.
2. Steal the crown jewels, which are very low in saturated fat but quite high in fibre.
3. Steal the Mona Lisa, which has no added salt or sugar.

'I went for the fish, of course, because I was a fish lover. Well, I say a fish lover, but I wasn't too keen on haddock,' continued the ghost 'but I would have eaten it if there was nothing else going.'

Longstint was finding it hard to believe he was having a conversation about fish with a ghost with a centre parting, but decided to find out more.

'What is your name?' he asked.

'Since I became a ghost my name has been Lawrence,' the ghost replied.

'What was it before you were a ghost?' Longstint enquired.

'Lawrence,' replied Lawrence the ghost. 'I won't get a spirit name until I've passed my exams.'

Longstint asked Lawrence if he had decided what to call himself when he passed his exams, and he replied 'Lawrence.'

With that, Longstint gave up asking questions.

Lawrence then informed Longstint and Zamborina that he had to take twenty tins of pilchards to pass this stage of the exam.

Longstint thought for a while and decided that another ten tins to go with the ones he had taken from Krowfin would not really leave the Willigrews short (not that they were tall, at all), and that he would help Lawrence carry the pilchards outside.

Before very long Lawrence and the two Willigrews had carried the tins and placed them behind a bush.

Lawrence explained that when his spirit examiner, Mrs Mary Scary who is a bit hairy, came, she would change the pilchards into phantom fish, and they would take them back to the other side, wherever that was.

Lawrence thanked the pair for their help and said it was time for him to go. This made the little Willigrews a bit sad because they had grown quite fond of their spooky friend with the centre parting.

Before he went, Longstint asked Lawrence about the next question in the exam.

'Next,' said Lawrence, 'I have got to find a fairly tall creature and make it jump with fright.'

The Willigrews wished him luck and, with a wave of his hand, Lawrence started to disappear, his feet at first, then his legs and, finally, his centre parting.

Longstint sat for a while pondering, well we all ponder sometimes, and he thought of how he would tell the rest of his tribe about Lawrence the trainee ghost. Zamborina said she would help him explain.

They sat for a while gathering their thoughts, put them in a little pile on a table, and then started to sort them into some sort of order.

They thought of the second thing that happened and decided that the first thing that happened must go before that.

The rest was easy, the fourth thing came after the third thing, and the seventh thing came two after the fifth thing and two before the ninth thing.

'Sorted and wrapped,' Zamborina said, loudly, which made Longstint jump a bit.

The next morning when all the chickweed

tea and all the cake had gone, the two little ghost watchers went to Bronglay's house to tell him what had happened.

When they arrived, they saw that a small crowd had gathered, anxious to hear about the pilchards.

Bronglay was already at the door and invited everybody in.

'Come in everybody,' he said. (See, I told you so), and, not surprisingly, everybody entered Bronglay's house.

Bronglay had already prepared a nice cup of tea for the two Willigrews, who had watched over the pilchards, so they sat at the table and explained in some detail, what happened during the night.

'That's amazing,' said Yill, looking amazed. 'Were you in great danger?'

'Not really,' replied Zamborina. 'The ghost was a friendly cove who was just a bit confused. I don't think he'll be back, so our pilchards will be safe in future and Krowfin will get his Omega 3.'

All the Willigrews that were present praised Longstint and Zamborina for their bravery and for staying awake all night, which wasn't easy for a Willigrew.

Yill was so delighted at the news that she started doing the Willigrew dance, hopping about on one leg and flicking her earlobes with her fingers.

The others soon joined in and a merry time was had by all.

The End

THE WILLIGREWS AND THE NIGHT SHADOWS

As you may know, from previous stories about the Willigrews, the area around their village was full of all sorts of weird and wonderful creatures. Some were friendly; some were unfriendly and some were, of course, very unfriendly indeed.

There were some, however, who would have liked to be unfriendly but couldn't be asked, as they were too lazy. This story is about some spirits that were not only unfriendly, but also, intent on destroying the Willigrews and everything they held dear.

It all began one clear moonlit night as Dora Dingbat and Yill were sitting outside on the village green looking at the stars.

They had been sitting for some time, without speaking, when Dora said,' How many stars do you think there are Yill?'

'Oh, I don't know, I guess there must be thousands of them; I have tried counting them, you know, but my eyes always went funny, and I lost my focus,' replied Yill.

'I don't think your eyes are at all funny, Yill; they have never made me laugh anyway, and if I find your lost focus lying around somewhere, I'll know where to bring it,' joked Dora.

Dora was just about to stand up, to make her way home to bed, when Yill said, 'Did you see that, over there in the trees?'

'No,' replied Dora, 'what was it?'

'I thought I saw a shadow, moving about, it was probably nothing, or perhaps it was an animal or something,' said Yill.

'Oh yes, I see it now, sort of a purple colour, I wonder what it could be?' asked Dora.

Then they both jumped with surprise as the 'shadow' let out an eerie howl. 'HOWOOO,' it went, which made a shiver run down the Willigrews spines, the shiver carried on down there legs and scuttled off into the undergrowth.

'That doesn't sound like any animal I've ever heard,' said Dora, 'and look, there are more of them, must be a dozen or so, we had better tell Bronglay.'

The shadows seemed to be floating in and around the trees, like swirling misty beings swooping in and out, fading away and reappearing. All the time there came the weird, spooky howling.

At Bronglay's house, he was just getting ready for bed and making himself and Yill a drink of milky chickweed tea.

'Ah, there you are my little fluffy one, and hello Dora, did you spot any interesting stars tonight?' said Bronglay.

'No, not really,' Yill replied, 'but we have seen something a little disturbing and think you might like to take a look.'

Bronglay followed Yill and Dora out to where they had seen the shadows and Yill pointed to where they had been. There was no activity at all in the trees so the Willigrews started to go home, when Bronglay spotted the purple shadows in a group of trees further along.

'There back,' he said, pointing, 'this is all a bit weird; I think we should call out Longstint and Krowfin and, of course, Partive and Parsleno.'

When the others arrived, Bronglay asked everyone to be quiet, and to wait to see what the shadows did.

As they were watching, one of the misty creatures came to the forest edge and, as it did, the purple mist formed into the blurred shape of a face. They were all watching so intently that nobody noticed Longstint who, eyes wide open, was walking toward the face.

He seemed in a trance and was getting very close when the shadow spoke, 'Come with us, we are your friends and we need you,' it said, in a whispering ghostly voice.

Longstint was in a sort of dream, as if hypnotised by the voice, which called him on. However, just in time, Dora noticed Longstint and ran over to him, grabbed him by the shoulders and shook him vigorously, woke him from his trance, and led him back to the others.

Longstint was still a bit groggy and said, 'What happened, I felt a bit giddy, they said they were my friends and, for a moment, I believed them? Thank you Dora, I couldn't stop myself, it felt so strange.'

'No problem, Longstint my love, you would have done the same for me.' Dora replied.

'Right,' said Bronglay, 'we must now be very careful not to look into the shadows' eyes. They seem to have some sort of hypnotic power. We will leave Partive and Parsleno on guard overnight, and then have a meeting in the morning.'

Throughout the night, the shadows moved in and out of the trees, only disappearing when dawn broke.

'Well, dawn is breaking now, the shadows have gone,' said Partive, 'I suppose we should report back to Bronglay.

Parsleno agreed, but, on the way to Bronglay's house, he asked Partive a question, 'You know when dawn breaks, who repairs it? Only, it happens every day and it's always new in the morning.'

'Now, I have got a theory about that,' replied Partive, 'I think there is a group of creatures whose part-time job it is to repair the dawn every day. They are probably called 'The Dawn Repair Patrol.'

'Ah, that explains it then,' said Parsleno, totally convinced.

When the two night watchmen arrived at the Meeting Hall, quite a crowd had gathered. They were all, naturally, curious about the previous night's events.

Bronglay called them all to order and spoke:

'Morning everyone,' he began, 'no doubt you have all heard about last night's strange happenings. Purple shadowy things were seen in the trees, and we are worried that they may mean us harm. The most important warning I can issue is that you should not, under any circumstances, look into the eyes of these spirits or ghosts or whatever they are. They appear to have hypnotic powers and may tempt you to go into the trees. DO NOT GO WITH THEM!'

'Now I know that we Willigrews are inquisitive creatures and that some of you may wish to see the shadows, so those of you who are interested should assemble by the trees at midnight tonight. Make sure you only have a light dinner, because there will be jangleberry jam sandwiches and chickweed tea to sustain us through the night.'

'We have placed a barrier at what Partive considers to be a safe distance, so please do not cross it. Just to reassure you, I have arranged a meeting with Cload, to see if he knows anything about the shadows, and I will share his thoughts with you tonight.'

As you may know, from previous stories, Cload is the oldest living Willigrew. He is very wise and has a memory that is longer than his beard and shorter than his back garden.

He, Bronglay and Yill sat at the kitchen table in Bronglay's house, with a nice cup of chickweed tea.

'Ah, Brongers and Yillipops, my two favourite Willigrews,' said Cload, taking a slurp of his tea. 'I have heard about the purple shadows and wondered how I can help you?'

Yill replied, 'We wondered if you had heard of this sort of thing before Cload, you know, somewhere in the distant past?'

'Well,' responded Cload, 'before I decide I would like to see these strange things. Without seeing them in the flesh, so to speak, I would hazard a guess that they were some sort of wandering spirits.'

'Now, there are two kinds of restless spirits, the first kind are harmless enough and are just looking in on the real world in an attempt to frighten creatures like us for a bit of fun. The second kind, however, are probably looking for replacements for their spirits that have passed into another spirit zone. You see; they have to keep up their numbers by luring creatures to join them. I am worried that if one of the Willigrews actually succumbs to the hypnotic beckoning, and enters the mist, they will become one of the spirits and be lost forever.'

'What a dreadful thought,' said Yill, pouring out some more tea. 'Is there nothing we can do to frighten them off, Cload?'

'Don't worry Yill, when I see them, I will try to think of something,' said Cload reassuringly.

Quite a large crowd had gathered at midnight to get a look at the shadows. Partive and Parsleno manned the barrier, to make sure nobody crossed the line.

Suddenly, a cry went up, it was Krowfin, 'They're back,' he shouted, pointing.

Everything went quiet as the shadows started dancing through the trees again and making that spooky howling sound, 'HOWOOO,' they went. This time more of the shadows formed themselves into ghostly grotesque faces, which seemed to leave there bodies and move, threateningly to the edge of the trees.

Yill noticed that the faces had no real features, just holes where the eyes and mouths should have been. Then the beckoning began, 'Come with us, we are your friends and we need you.'

'Do not look into their eyes,' shouted Bronglay, 'just stay where you are, and you should be safe.'

He need not have worried because everybody's eyes turned to see something running along the tree line.

It was a muntjac deer. It ran in front of the shadows, but when it saw the Willigrews, it turned sharp left.

Longstint shouted, 'Stop little deer,' but it was too late. The unfortunate creature ran straight into the shadows. Within seconds, the deer was submerged in a purple mist; it made no sound and disappeared as the shadows started howling in triumph.

'Poor little dear,' cried Krowfin, tearfully, 'we must make sure that doesn't happen to any of us.'

Bronglay told Cload, who had just arrived, the sad news about the deer. Yill brought a chair for Cload, and he sat down to study the shadows.

After about ten minutes, he called Bronglay over and said, 'I am sorry to tell you, old chap, but these are the worst sort of spirits. This is what I was dreading, these evil things are called Willtakers, because they take away their victim's will to resist.'

'Why don't you try your magic Bronglay?' asked Yill, 'it sounds like our last chance.'

'Well, I'll give it a try, it might work,' replied Bronglay.

'I doubt it will work on these spirits,'

warned Cload, 'they exist in a different place, not just a parallel existence, but a higher plain.'

'OK,' said Bronglay, 'I'll give it a try anyway.'

Then he started to think of a rhyme to help his magic to work.

He began:

Go purple spirits,
And leave us alone,
We mean you no harm,
But wish you were gone.

If you don't come back,
For a million years,
It will be much too soon,
So please disappear.

The Willtakers suddenly went very quiet, so the Willigrews thought something was about to happen. Had Bronglay's magic worked?

Everyone crossed their fingers and waited, but nothing happened and, after a few minutes, the spirits started howling again.

'What now,' asked Bronglay, to nobody in particular?

'There is one other who may be able to help us,' said Cload. 'There is a mobile wizard called Magicnose the Witchman, who is very powerful. I know where he lives; I think he is on holiday at the moment, so he shouldn't be out on his rounds.'

Cload assured Bronglay that the tribe would probably be safe until the wizard came, because he didn't think the Willtakers could come out of the trees.

He also said that their powers only worked on the weakness of others and that the Willigrews must keep remembering not to look into their eyes and to stay strong.

Leaving Partive and Parsleno to watch the Willtakers, Bronglay, Longstint, Krowfin, Dora and, of course, Cload made their way to Magicnose's house.

It wasn't that far, about half the distance it would have been, had it been twice as far as it was.

The little group were making their way through the forest, following a narrow path between some high bushes, when Dora said, 'I just love bushes,'

'Why do you love bushes in particular Dora?' asked Krowfin.

'Well,' replied Dora, 'because they are not trees and they are not grass.'

'But they are not sandwiches either,' commented Longstint.

'Of course they're not sandwiches Longstint, that would be a silly reason for liking something,' said Dora.

Not even trying to understand Dora's logic, the rest carried on without speaking, until, that is, they came to a small caravan in a clearing in the forest.

'This is it,' said Cload, 'Magicnose's house, I'll see if he is in.'

Cload rang the bell that played a little tune, which got Dora and Krowfin dancing a very small jig, which the others ignored.

'Come in, Cload old fellow, can you put the kettle on, I'm gasping for a cup of tea?' shouted Magicnose.

When the Willigrews entered the caravan, they were surprised to see Magicnose in bed, with his leg up in a sort of slingy thing.

'Hello Magicnose old chap, what have you been up to?' asked Cload, looking a bit concerned.

'My knee caught fire,' explained Magicnose, 'spontaneous combustion, it's an occupational hazard I'm afraid. I was casting a particularly strong spell, to rid a small gentleman's right ear of poltergeist, and the power went straight to my left knee. I managed to put it out fairly quickly, but it hurt quite a bit.'

'That is terrible,' gasped Dora, 'you poor wizard.'

'Oh! Don't worry,' said Magicnose, with a reassuring smile, 'it could have been much worse. One of my wizardy friends, Maurice the Magician, was casting a spell once, and his knee exploded, so I was pretty lucky. Now, enough about me, to what do I owe this visit from so many lovely Willigrews?'

'We were hoping you could help us with a Willtaker problem we are having,' said Cload, 'Bronglay has tried his magic, without success, and they have already taken a muntjac deer.'

'Oh dear,' (no pun intended) replied Magicnose, 'how sad, it is one of life's little ironies that the most harmless among us always seem to suffer the most harm. Willtakers, you say, they are a very powerful force and not easy to get rid of. However, the Willigrews have always been good to me, so I will do my best to help you.'

Krowfin handed Magicnose a cup of tea,

and he sat on the edge of his bed.

He was already dressed, from head to foot in shiny purple clothes.

As he draped a purplish cloak around his shoulders, he said, 'now for the finishing touch,' as he placed a very tall, very purple, very pointy wizard's hat on his head.

'But what about your poor knee,' asked Dora, 'will you be able to walk that far?'

'Oh, I am sure I will be OK, if you help me,' replied Magicnose.

Therefore, when the wizard was ready, the little group started the short journey back to Willigrew.

On the way, Longstint had a question for Magicnose. 'Why don't you cast a spell on your knee, in order to heal it?' he asked.

'Good question,' replied the wizard, 'I certainly would if I could remember the spell. You see I can remember the spell for burnt right knees, but the spell for left knees has escaped my mind. I had it written down somewhere, but I simply can't find it. I am afraid it will just have to heal naturally. I have, of course, put some left knee burn ointment on, so that should help.'

It wasn't long before the five Willigrews and one wizard arrived back in Willigrew.

Bronglay reported straight to Partive and Parsleno, who informed him that nothing much had happened in their absence and that most of the other Willigrews had stayed away from the trees, for fear of being tempted.

Bronglay walked over to the trees and saw that the purple shadows were still there, howling and flitting in and out of the branches. Someone brought a chair for Magicnose and placed it a few metres from the tree line.

The wizard approached and walked past the chair and almost right up to purple shadows. This seemed to upset the Willtakers, who started to swirl around howling and almost screaming the words, 'we are your friends, come with us now, we need you.'

'Right then, my little pretties,' said Magicnose defiantly, 'let us see your faces, or are you too cowardly to look upon the mighty Witchman?'

Almost immediately, a large purple face thrust forward to within a few centimetres of the wizard's nose. Magicnose looked directly into the shadows eyes.

'Oh! No,' gasped Yill, 'he will be taken; he is looking into its eyes. Shall we bring him back before they hypnotise him, I can't watch.'

'Just wait a few moments; I think he knows what he is doing,' advised Bronglay.

The Willtaker stared at Magicnose and Magicnose stared at the Willtaker. The suspense was terrible, who would blink first?

Suddenly, the shadow gave out an ear-piercing howl and projected a stream of foul-smelling purple slime from the place where its nose should be, directly at the wizards face.

Magicnose, without diverting his eyes, moved calmly to one side.

The slime squirted over his shoulder, landing behind him on the grass, which immediately, hissed, then shrivelled up and died.

'OK then, Willtaker, so you want to play rough do you?' fumed Magicnose, as he pulled out his most powerful weapon, his wand, which he waved, threateningly at the shadow.

He then began to chant a spell, which went quite a bit like this:

'Umbra, umbram, uanescet. et non revertuntur ad nos relinquere, Ite, ite in orbe peaced.' Then repeated the last few words, in a whisper, 'Ite, ite in orbe peaced.'

The Willtaker gave out a loud, despairing

howl, which had all the Willigrews covering their ears. Magicnose moved even closer, almost touching, the shadow and stared harder.

Then, to everyone's amazement, the shadow moved back, the expression on its face softened, as if in relief. The other shadows started to float upward, disappearing as they went.

Eventually the large shadow turned its face back to Magicnose and said, 'Thank you mighty wizard, you have set us free.'

The last Willtaker started to rise into the treetops, finally disappearing in a cloud of purple mist.

The Willigrews cheered and started their dance of hopping about on one leg and flicking their earlobes with their index fingers.

'Let's hear it for the wizard,' shouted Longstint, and everyone chanted, 'Wizard, wizard, you' the man, you' the man!'

Their celebrations were cut short, however, when Yill gasped, 'Oh No! Look, look, the mist is back!'

Everyone looked to the trees with open mouths and ears pointing in different directions; the mist was indeed back.

What followed, however, delighted the Willigrews, as out of the mist there came a small animal; it was the muntjac deer, unharmed. It ran back along the tree line, to freedom.

An even bigger cheer went up.

More chanting arose from the Willigrews, 'Muntjac, muntjac, you' the deer, you' the deer.'

Bronglay thanked Magicnose and gave him a cup of chickweed tea and some jangleberry dodgy jammers, which he munched and slurped gratefully.

The Willtakers who, hopefully, had gone back to their higher plane, never visited Willigrew again; and the village settled back to normality.

The End

THE WILLIGREWS AND THE MIGHTY STUMP OF DOOM

This story is about a tree stump, probably an oak tree that has long since been chopped down.

To us humans it wasn't all that big, but to the Willigrews, being as they are, so very small, it was enormous, all of two metres high and about six metres around its base.

The Mighty Stump of Doom, as the Willigrews called it, was like a very high mountain, which had never been climbed.

For some time, some of the tribe had wondered what the view was like from the top of the stump. They wondered and wondered until one day as Longstint and Rewsin were returning from a hard day's work on the chickweed beds they talked about how difficult it would be to climb.

'I was wondering,' said Longstint, 'how difficult it would be to climb The Mighty Stump of Doom.'

'Very difficult, I would imagine.' replied Rewsin. 'The other brave Willigrews that tried never returned, and don't forget all the stories about the strange beasts that live up there.'

Anyway, they both agreed that it would be a great adventure, and that they should ask their leader Bronglay for permission to organise an expedition.

They went straight to Bronglay's house (well, actually they had to turn a couple of corners) and knocked on the door.

Yill came to the door and welcomed the two little chaps in by saying, 'Welcome you two little chaps.'

'Hello Yill is Bronglay in?' they asked.

'Yes, he's in the lounge practising his snoring,' she replied.

As they entered, Bronglay was making a loud snorting sound. He looked at Rewsin and Longstint and asked, 'What do think of that for a snore, good or what?'

'That's an excellent snore,' said Rewsin, 'have you got any more.'

In reply, Bronglay put one finger in his left nostril, stood on one leg, held his other hand above his head and let out what was really a high-pitched purring, whistley sound.

'Absolute classic snore,' shouted Longstint, excitedly.

'Much respect,' said Rewsin in agreement.

'Well, enough of that,' said Bronglay; 'what can I do for you chaps?'

Rewsin began 'We are thinking of trying to climb the Mighty Stump of Doom,' he said, 'and we would like your advice and, of course, your permission.'

'Hold on a minute,' gasped Bronglay, 'that would be a very dangerous thing to do. Have you thought it through, seriously? Why would you want to risk your lives on such a perilous mission?'

Rewsin answered first, saying that he liked to face challenges in his life and that to succeed would be a great honour and would enhance The Willigrews reputation throughout the known world.

Longstint followed this with 'It might be a bit of fun.'

Bronglay explained to the two brave little Willigrews that he would like some time to think about their idea and that he would let them know in the morning or tomorrow, whichever comes first.

With that, Rewsin and Longstint said goodbye and went off to make their plans; hoping the answer would be yes.

Bronglay decided to discuss things with Yill. He always did this when he had a problem.

He said to Yill, 'I would like to discuss a problem with you, my lovely little green furry dumpling.'

'What's the problem, my handsome little green fluff-ball?' asked Yill.

'Well, it's like this,' Bronglay continued, 'Rewsin and Longstint have come up with a plan to climb The Mighty Stump of Doom and have asked for my permission.'

'Well, that is a problem,' she said. 'That would be very, very dangerous, as you know, several Willigrews have tried and never returned.'

The names of the adventurers who went up The Stump were inscribed on a large stone on the village green, with this message.

In Memory of the Brave Willigrews Who Tried to Climb The Mighty Stump of Doom

Vodrabo
Dornig
Enog
Colmanda
Benmanda
Nostrilgaw

If they never return, we will see them when they do

In addition, there were some scary rumours about creatures that lived in the dense forests that covered the 'Stump'.

Some said that a fierce dragon lived near the top, others that a wicked witch with bad dress sense and even badder breath lived in the lichen forest.

Another story told of a mad sausage man that could turn your nose purple and lived in a cave about half way up.

There were nice stories, however, about a kindly fairy who was so beautiful, she could make the sun blush and an equally beautiful princess who was so sparkly and pink she could turn night into day, but not at weekends, when she had to charge up her sparkles using solar panels, which she carried in her handbag.

After much discussion, walking over to the window and back, standing on one leg while scratching the other and making small clicky noises with their tongues, Bronglay and Yill decided to let Rewsin and Longstint attempt to climb The Mighty Stump of Doom.

I am glad they did or this story would have ended here.

Next morning, when Rewsin and Longstint arrived Bronglay opened the door to greet them. They looked half-nervous and half-excited. Their top halves were excited and their bottom halves were nervous.

Bronglay said he would give them permission to go, but that they must promise him that the moment they felt that their lives were in danger they must turn around and come back to Willigrew. He explained that they would still be heroes, even if they tried and failed.

The two would-be adventurers were overjoyed.

'Whoop, whoop!' shouted Longstint. 'Ditto, ditto!' agreed Rewsin.

That afternoon a meeting was held in the Big Hall, which had been built recently to hold important meetings.

A medium sized hall had also been built for less important meetings and a really small one for discussing what they were having for dinner and what the weather was going to be like.

The meeting was to discuss plans for the expedition and was attended by Rewsin, Longstint, Bronglay, Yill, Krowfin, Vectorn and Father.

Bronglay was first to speak.

'To begin with,' he said, 'I would like to make an announcement. Rewsin and Longstint have asked my permission, which I have given, to attempt to climb The Mighty Stump of Doom. I realise that this will be very dangerous, very perilous and a bit hairy, but I feel they deserve the chance to give it a try.'

Krowfin said 'Ooer!'

Vectorn said, 'Too risky!'

And Father said, 'Is there any tea going?'

A list was made of the equipment that would be needed on the trip and this is that very list:

Warm clothing

Cold clothing

Plenty of chickweed tea

Lots of food

Two sleeping bags

Two waking bags

More chickweed tea

A small piece of wood in the shape of a bat's ear, which Krowfin had found the day before and thought, although not very useful, might bring them luck.

The very next morning, having gathered all the equipment together, Longstint and Rewsin met at the 'thirty tree'.

A large crowd of well-wishers had gathered to say goodbye to the two little green, furry adventurers.

Some of the crowd were carrying banners saying things like, 'Good luck chaps', 'Keep safe', and 'Wish I was coming with you'.

One banner said, 'Good luck Bronglay and

Krowfin'.

Repscar, who had saved it from a previous adventure and didn't have time to make a new one, carried this.

As the two started out in the direction of The Stump the crowd cheered and waved their hands in the air.

Everyone waved except Yill who was sad to see them go, looking so small and helpless, and about to face many dangers.

So, as she usually did, she recited a little rhyme, which went something like this:

Go boldly little Willigrews,
And you will be all right,
But remember that by night it's dark,
And that by day it's light.

You know there may be dangers,
But then there may be none,
So if you find yourselves confused,
Just eat a chickweed bun.

If you should find you miss us,
And I should think you will,
Keep strong and think of Willigrew,
Cos' we'll be waiting still.

Before long Longstint and Rewsin disappeared into the distance and all the other Willigrews went back home.

As they walked along, side by side, Rewsin turned to Longstint and said, 'Well this is it mate, we are on our way to conquer The Mighty Stump of Doom, are you excited or frightened?'

'Well,' replied Longstint, 'part of me is frightened and part of me is excited.'

They didn't discuss which parts.

For a while, the journey was fairly uneventful, until up ahead they spotted someone sitting at the side of the path.

There before them, sitting on a tree stump, was a really weird looking creature.

Most of its body was smooth and leathery, like, well, smooth leathery stuff. Its face was round and red with a few tufts of hair here and there. Its body was quite small, but the strangest thing was that although it was sitting on the stump its backside was resting on the ground behind it. It was huge, quivering and glistening in the morning sun.

Before the Willigrews could say hello the creature greeted them with a big smile.

'Good morning to you, I am Wobobble of the

Wobblybum tribe. Who do I have the pleasure of meeting?' it said.

'Good grief,' thought Longstint, 'his name must be Wobobble Wobblybum!'

'I am called Longstint and this is my friend Rewsin,' answered Longstint. 'We are from the Willigrew tribe, you may have heard of us.'

'Indeed I have,' replied Wobobble. 'Our leader, Bobble, has told us many good things about your tribe and you are highly respected for being peace-loving, brave and all round pretty good types in a general way.'

'Well, thank you,' said Rewsin. 'It is a pleasure to meet you. We are on our way to try to climb to the top of The Mighty Stump of Doom.'

Wobobble's eyes widened, his mouth fell open and his bum wobbled.

'The Mighty Stump of Doom,' he gasped, 'did you say The Mighty Stump of Doom?'

'Er, yes.' Longstint replied. 'Could you point us in the right direction?'

'Well, I'll take you part of the way, gladly, but I will go no further than the fuzzy boodad trees!' continued Wobobble.

Then he started to speak with a strange accent, sort of West Country, with a hint of Long John Silver.

'Folk around these parts say that once you go past the boodad trees, strange things do 'appen. They tell of evil goings on and doings. Strange sounds and screams and loud burps do be 'eard!'

'Well, thanks for the warning,' said Rewsin, 'but we are the tribe that faced the nasty Gloopudds, so we will carry on, regardless of the dangers.'

Wobobble replied, 'Well don't say I didn't warn you.'

So they didn't.

Wobobble asked the Willigrews to follow

him closely and warned again of the dangers they would face on the Stump.

He went ahead, walking quite slowly. His wobbly bottom dragging on the ground, although when he speeded up his bottom sort of bounced along. The Willigrews followed close behind.

As they walked, Wobobble sang a little song:

We are the Wobblybums,
And our bums they do wobble,
As we walk along,
They wibble and they wobble.

They wibble and they wobble,
They wobble and they wibble,
When they're not wibbling their wobbling,
When they're not wobbling their wibbling.

Our leader is called Bobble,
We answer to his call,
Because we know, he has,
The biggest bum of all.

They wibble and they wobble,
They wobble and they wibble,
When they're not wibbling their wobbling,
When they're not wobbling their wibbling.

The three little creatures walked for about half a kilometre until they saw, up ahead, a small group of trees.

'Them's the fuzzy boodad trees,' said Wobobble, 'I'll go no further, but wish you luck, which I am sure you will need.'

Rewsin and Longstint thanked their new friend and walked into the clump of trees. As they went further in, the air seemed to get colder and the light started to fade.

'It's a bit scary in here, isn't it?' said Rewsin, nervously.

'Too right,' replied Longstint, 'I hope it isn't too far to The Mighty Stump of Doom.'

No sooner had he spoken than something emerged from the trees to their right and, in an instant, disappeared into the trees on their left. The thing moved so quickly it was difficult to make it out, but it was dark, very large and blurry.

Longstint asked Rewsin, 'Did you see that dark, very large and blurry thing just then?'

'I did,' his friend replied, frozen to the spot, with fear.

'We had better hurry past in case it comes back,' advised Longstint, lifting Rewsin from the frozen spot he was standing on and urging him onward, deeper into the trees.

They both decided they should run for a bit, not because they were frightened at all, but that the exercise would warm them up. So they ran for a while, too nervous to look back, until they came to a small green gate blocking their way.

As they got nearer to the gate, they heard a whistling sound coming from above them. Looking up they saw, sitting on a low branch, a small bird. It was sort of brown with a grey head and looked a bit 'twitchy'. Then, to their surprise, it spoke.

'Wotcha, you two,' it chirped. 'We don't often see strangers in these parts, especially furry, green strangers.'

'We are not strangers, we know each other,' replied Rewsin, sniffily. (Well he was just getting over a nasty cold and didn't have a handkerchief).

'Sorry I'm sure,' said the little bird. 'Let me introduce myself. My name is Duffy from the Scrunnock tribe, and I have been sent by your tour company to be your guide on the perilous journey you are about to embark upon on this auspicious occasion. I will also be providing you with holiday insurance and currency exchange, commission-free, of course.'

'He does go on a bit,' remarked Rewsin.

'I do go on a bit,' said Duffy, cheerily, 'it's what we Scrunnocks do.'

'And, if you don't mind my asking, why are you so nervous and twitchy all the time?' Rewsin continued.

'Well,' answered Duffy. 'The natural enemy of the Scrunnocks is the Harrow Spawk. They are much bigger than us, with hooky beaks and sharp pointy talons! The Harrow Spawks look on Scrunnocks as tasty snacks. So, you see, I am always on the lookout out for an attack from above.'

The Willigrews then introduced themselves

to Duffy Scrunnock and started toward the green gate, which swung open as they approached.

Duffy flew on ahead and the Willigrews followed, feeling reassured, now that they had someone to show them the way through the trees.

Having walked what must have been the major part of a fairly long way, they came upon a sign, which read:

ATTENTION!
HERE THERE BE LOBECHOMPERS!
IN THE EVENT OF AN ATTACK, EAR
LOBES SHOULD BE COVERED, AND
KNEES SLIGHTLY BENT

The trio carried on their way for a while, keeping a look out for Lobechompers, when, as they turned a corner in the path, there, before them, stood The Mighty Stump of Doom. Rewsin gasped as he surveyed the huge tree stump.

'Wow, it's enormous!' he said, a bit shakily.

Longstint was speechless, so he didn't say anything, he just stood and stared in silence.

Duffy could see the Willigrews were a bit

shocked, so advised them to stop for the night and start the climb in the morning after they had rested.

Rewsin prepared some chickweed burgers and a nice cup of chickweed tea, and the two settled down in the shelter of a bush at the edge of the trees. Duffy settled on a tree branch for the night having declined an offer of food, saying that he always saved a juicy Jangleberry for supper.

As they sat, munching away and slurping their tea, Longstint asked, 'Well, what do you think tomorrow will hold, Rewsin?'

'I don't know,' replied Rewsin. 'But one thing I do know is that we'll be all right as long as we stick together, as Willigrews always do.'

Soon, both Willigrews fell asleep to the sound of Duffy, snoring from the tree above.

The night passed quietly, and, in the morning, as dawn broke Rewsin stretched then set about making some breakfast, which consisted of toast with jangleberry jam and chickweed tea.

As Longstint awoke, Duffy fluttered down from his tree branch and sang a little twittery song, he said, 'to greet the morning.'

'Right,' said Duffy. 'This is your last chance to change your minds and turn back.'

The Willigrews, however, decided that they would keep the minds they had, and continue their journey.

'Are you quite sure?' asked the little bird, 'because, if you turn back after this point you will be going the wrong way.'

The three adventurers eventually reached the foot of the Stump, which looked even higher close up.

Duffy flew a short way up, sat on a ledge, and shouted to the others to climb up to him.

As this part of the stump was not too steep, the climb was fairly easy. On reaching the ledge, they noticed a small opening, which was slightly overgrown with moss.

'Fancy taking a look inside?' asked Longstint.

'OK by me,' replied Rewsin, bravely.

As they entered the opening, it widened out into a large cave.

'Is there anybody home?' shouted Longstint, not expecting a reply.

However, an answer did come, from deeper in the cave. 'No, I'm not in. I went out for the day to buy a book on interior decorating for the small cave,' said a female voice, which sounded a bit cross.

'But you must be in,' said Rewsin, 'because we can hear you.'

'This isn't me,' the voice argued, 'this is a recorded message.'

Longstint was confused, but Rewsin wasn't. They ventured further into the cave and, after looking behind several rocks, found a little creature hiding.

The creature was easy to spot because her head was hidden, but her bottom was sticking out.

'There you are,' said Rewsin.

'How can you see me if I can't see you?' asked the voice.

Why don't you come out and meet us?' Rewsin asked, reassuringly. We are Willigrews, so will not harm you.'

'Oh, all right then,' came the grudging reply, 'but I'm not officially here, so don't tell anyone you've seen me.'

There followed a scuffling sound, and, out from behind a rock came a small, spiky thing that looked like a cross between a hedgehog and a hamster!

The small spiky thing spoke again. 'All right then, wodja want? I haven't got all day to stand around talking to you, I have better things to do with my life, like standing on my head and singing lovely songs about fish, I'll have you know it is ages since I did that.'

'We are very sorry,' said Longstint, 'we were just curious; we didn't mean to disturb you.'

'I don't know,' complained the spiky thing, 'you're minding your own business, in your own little cave, and all sorts of creatures come stomping around in your home being all green and furry. What's the world coming to?'

The two Willigrews, realising that they

were not welcome, started back out toward the cave exit. As they left, they heard the little spiky thing grumbling away and then singing this song.

I love fish, cos they are lovely things,
Oh! Yes fish are very nice because they don't
have wings,
I love fish and if I had a wish,
I'd use that wish and ask to be a fish.

The Willigrews carried on their journey, chuckling as they went.

'What was all that about?' asked Longstint.

'Don't ask me,' replied Rewsin. 'It's a funny old world, and no mistake.'

Duffy Scrunnock, who flew down and perched on a rock, then greeted them.

'I see you're back then,' said the little bird.

'Not much gets past you, does it Duffy?' joked Longstint, and all three of them laughed.

Nothing much happened for a while, although they did think they saw the blurry shape again, which was a bit scary. It seemed to be following them.

'I'll fly ahead,' said Duffy, 'to see what's further up the mountain.'

After a while, he returned, looking more twitchy and nervous than ever.

'Look out,' he squealed, 'there's a mad chipolata up ahead, half man half frankfurter, it's gruesome, all sweaty and pink, help, call the police, call the fire brigade, call a plumber, call a landscape gardener, call several different trades people! I want my mum.'

'Good grief,' exclaimed Longstint, 'Duffy's lost the plot.'

Rewsin ran over to Duffy and put a hand on his wing, it was Longstint's hand.

'Calm down, little feathery chap,' he said, 'you're hyperventilating, take a deep breath, or you'll pass out.'

Then turning to Longstint he said, 'Have you got a paper bag in your pocket?'

'I haven't even got a pocket,' replied Longstint.

Duffy, eventually, calmed down and got his breath back, he remembered where he'd left it.

'I advise you very strongly not to go any higher,' warned Duffy. 'That is the scariest looking creature I have ever seen, even in my reasonably uneventful life.'

'Wait a minute,' said Rewsin, 'that sounds like the sausage man we heard about, in the rumours.'

'Is that the one that turns your nose purple?' enquired Longstint, looking concerned.

'Must be,' answered Rewsin. 'I don't fancy a purple nose. I don't think that would be a very good look for a fashionable Willigrew.'

After much discussion, the three little mountaineers decided that it would be a shame to give up the expedition just because of purple noses, so they proceeded with caution.

Caution had just joined them and decided to walk with them for a while.

When they reached the sausage man, they were relieved to find him curled up, fast asleep, at the side of the track.

'Quickly,' advised Duffy, 'while he's curled up like a Cumberland sausage, you could run past him, before he wakes up.'

The Willigrews acted immediately. Sprinting at top speed, as fast as they could, they passed the sausage man, in double quick time.

When they had reached what they thought was a safe distance, they turned to look back. The sausage man had awoken, and was looking up the track toward them. However, he didn't seem to want to chase them, so they carried on up the track.

'We were lucky there,' sighed Longstint, in relief.

'You were not,' said Duffy, swooping down toward them, 'you've both got purple noses!'

The Willigrews looked at each other and gasped. Then they looked at Duffy and exclaimed, 'and you've got a purple beak!'

'Oh! No,' cried Duffy, 'I'll look all exotic, like some parrot from foreign parts, or something. What am I going to do?'

The other two tried to reassure the little bird by telling him that the purple effect might wear off after a while and that he'd soon be back to normal.

'Let's look on the bright side,' said Rewsin, 'our noses could have turned beige, which is so last year. I mean, purple might turn out to be this year's black, fashion-wise.'

Duffy didn't seem convinced but agreed to carry on anyway.

So off the little threesome went, taking their purple noses with them.

By now, it was beginning to get dark, so they decided to stop for the night, under a clump of dead moss, which was dry and warm.

They brewed up some chickweed tea and made a supper of chickweed scones with lashings of jangleberry jam.

As they sat, munching and slurping, Rewsin asked Longstint, 'Well, I wonder what tomorrow holds for us, old furry friend.'

'I don't know,' replied Longstint, 'but I hope it doesn't involve any more colour changes to any of our body parts.'

They then settled down for the night, curled up, and went to sleep, snoring through their purple noses.

Duffy sat on a tree, tucked his purple beak under his wing and drifted off for the night.

They all slept soundly, unaware of the dark blurry thing, that was watching from the shadows, waiting to make its move. Not hearing the low growling sound it made as it watched them with its piercing blood-red eyes.

Next morning bright and early, the Willigrews awoke to the sound of Duffy singing and chirruping his little head off.

'Oh, I wish I didn't have to do that dawn chorus stuff,' he complained, 'it always gives me such a headache.'

'Sounds fine to me,' said Longstint, yawning, stretching, and scratching his furry green armpit.

'Me too,' agreed Rewsin.

After having some breakfast, the little band of adventurers carried on upward until they came to a sign, which read:

WELCOME STRANGERS, YOU ARE ABOUT
TO ENTER THE REALM OF PRINCESS
TABITHA.
PREPARE TO BE REASONABLY
IMPRESSED BY HER STUNNING BEAUTY

After walking a bit further, the Willigrews were surprised by a large beetle, dressed in military uniform, and blowing a long horn very loudly.

'Visitors approaching, your highness,' it said, 'they look like two small gooseberries on legs, and they have a flappy thing with them, shall I let them pass?'

The Willigrews were miffed, so was Duffy.

'We're miffed,' complained Longstint (see, I told you they were miffed). 'We are Willigrews and are not related to gooseberries in any way!'

Then, to the Willigrews' amazement, the ground began to lighten with a rosy glow. Soft music began to play, and the sun shone much more brightly and, there before them, stood an amazingly beautiful figure, dressed entirely in pink silk.

Her eyes were big and round. On her head, which was covered in curly fair hair down to her shoulders, she wore a coronet, which was so sparkly it almost blinded the Willigrews.

Seeing Rewsin shielding his eyes, the princess said, 'Sorry, I will turn my sparkles down a bit for you.'

'Thank you, your great majestiness,' said Rewsin.

'Thank you indeed, your high pinkness,' added Longstint, bowing a bit.

The princess then said, 'Welcome, strangers, I am Princess Tabitha, and I am so pleased that you have come to visit me in my princessdom. I hope you will stay for a while, it's nearly breakfast time, and we are having royal sausage and regal chips.'

Longstint didn't fancy the idea of having chips for breakfast, but the sausages persuaded him.

'We would be most honoured to breakfast with you, your most high ladyness,' he said.

'There is no need to stand on ceremony with me, little ones,' she continued. 'Most people call me Tabs. I may be astonishingly beautiful and extremely regal, but I am really 'down with the kids.'

The guard then showed them to a huge round table, laden with large bowls of sausages and chips. The Willigrews washed their hands in the silver bowls provided and began to eat the food.

When Princess Tabitha joined them, Longstint and Rewsin stopped eating and stood up, until they were asked to sit down again.

'Now then,' 'You must tell me all about yourselves?' asked Princess Tabitha. 'Where are you from, to which tribe do you belong, but, most important of all, why have you ventured into this dangerous place?'

'We are from a village called Willigrew,' explained Longstint. 'Our tribe is called the Willigrews and being a tribe that likes to explore, we thought we would see what was at the top of this mountain.'

'Well, I hope you are prepared for all the perils that lie ahead,' warned the Princess. 'I see from your purple noses that you have already met the Sausage Man. However, mark my words carefully, brave Willigrews, there are much greater dangers ahead, and I can only protect you while you are in my princessdom!'

'Oh, I almost forgot, if you see a fairy called Chloe would you give her this recipe for me. It's for Jumbly Dumplings, and do please give her my royal regards.'

'We will, of course, and thank you for your kindness Tabs, but we must go on,' said Rewsin.

They finished their meal with noble scones, majestic honey and stately cream, then ventured forth (or was it fifth?), accompanied by the guard, who marched beside them saying 'left, right, left, right'.

The guard told the Willigrews that they would be safe until they reached the enchanted turnip plant, because no evil being could enter Her Pinkness' realm, then they must proceed unprotected.

Just as they saw the turnip plant up ahead, Duffy returned, sat on Longstint's shoulder and said, 'Sorry I had to leave you for a while, chaps, I had an appointment with the Head Scrunnock, to see about getting a promotion to deputy head Scrunnock. The interview went very well, and she said she would let me know in the next few days.'

They welcomed Duffy back, and then approached the enchanted turnip plant. It didn't look all that enchanted, just an ordinary plant, until it started to flash with a glaring red light. Then to Rewsin's surprise, it spoke.

'Aha!' it said, 'fooled you. I am no ordinary vegetable. I was enchanted by the spell of the witch with bad dress sense and even badder breath.'

'She gave me the power to do great evil, but we turnips are fairly friendly, as vegetables go, and I have discovered how to do great good. If you each take one of my leaves you will possess the power to disappear for three and a half minutes. However, you can only use this power once. When you want to disappear, just turn around three times.'

The Willigrews thanked the turnip, gently picked the leaves, and carried on. No sooner had they stepped out of the Princess' realm, than it started to pour with rain followed by flashes of lightning and rumbles of thunder.

'Run for cover,' squealed Duffy. 'It's a thunder storm!'

'Oh, thanks for that,' replied Longstint, jokingly, 'I thought it was just a cool breeze.'

They soon found shelter in a cave carved into the bark of the wood.

'That was a bit sudden,' chirped Duffy, shaking his feathers to dry himself. 'I hope it doesn't last too long.'

Rewsin stood at the entrance to the cave, looking out at the rain. The others soon joined him and waited quietly for the storm to stop.

'I wonder,' Duffy pondered, 'why the rain always comes down, why doesn't it, sometimes, go up.'

'Who knows?' answered Longstint.

'Oh that'll be gravitational force,' said Rewsin, knowingly.

'Ah, I thought it might be,' said Duffy, who

then paused and asked, 'What's gravitational force, when it's not wearing its bed socks.'

'It's the attraction due to gravitation that the Earth or another astronomical object exerts on an object on or near its surface,' explained Rewsin.

'Well, I never,' said Duffy, 'I didn't know that, I'll never look at rain in the same way again. I'll probably close one eye and look at it in that way.'

Longstint was amazed that his little green mate knew that, but didn't say so, he just felt proud.

Then Longstint said, 'I think the rain sounds like music. If you listen carefully, it goes tinkle, tinkle, pitter-patter, patter pitter, tinkle patter, pitter tinkle.'

'Mm,' said Rewsin. 'Nice tune, but I don't think much of the lyrics.'

'All right, it needs work,' said Longstint, 'but you see what I mean.'

The others said they did.

The rain started to ease off, so they decided to carry on. The ground was very wet and sploshy, which the two Willigrews thought was fun.

They stamped their feet as they walked,

singing, 'Splishy, sploshy splash, splash, splish splosh splash, our fur is soggy, splish, splosh, splash.'

'Don't get too wet.' warned Duffy, 'You'll get a cold in your feet.'

The others were about to explain to Duffy that you can't get a cold in your feet, when Rewsin's big toe sneezed, so they kept quiet.

The journey hadn't been too bad so far, apart from a few minor hitches, but the Willigrews and Duffy would not be prepared for what was up ahead, as they approached the Mossy Forest.

It was dense and dark as they entered under the canopy and they had to push the branches away to get through. There was an air of danger in this strange place, and our little threesome could sense it.

At last, they came to a clearing. All was quiet, then, out of nowhere came a blinding flash, the ground shook and steam began to rise from the wet ground.

Then, as the dust cleared, standing before them was a terrifyingly ugly witch? She let out a huge cackling laugh followed by a high-pitched scream.

Her breath was so smelly that when she

screamed the Williligrews held their noses in disgust. As for her dress sense, she was wearing ice blue jeans under her black cloak, not a good look for any fashionable witch.

'Who dares enter my domain?' she croaked. 'How dare you, little insignificant green things? You will regret disturbing my snooze. I will curse you both and turn you into dinner plates.'

Having said this she took a broomstick from beneath her black robes and pointed it at the Williligrews.

Rewsin and Longstint shook with fear, they couldn't run, they were trapped!

The witch began her curse, 'Lumpkin,

dumpkin, waddling goose.' However, before she could finish Duffy flew bravely into her face, knocking her off her feet.

She rolled about on the ground, cursing and shouting at the little bird. She got to her feet and pointed the broomstick at Duffy who was coming in for a second attack.

'Don't do it Duffy,' warned Rewsin, but it was too late, a flash of blue light from the broomstick hit Duffy and he spiralled down, hitting the ground with a thump. He lay completely still.

'You killed our mate,' cried Longstint. 'You horrible, wicked witch, you'll pay for this!'

'Oh I will, will I?' the witch cackled, and pointed her broomstick once again.

She had just started with the Lumpkin, dumpkin stuff again, when Rewsin remembered the turnip leaves.

'Quick Longstint,' said Rewsin, urgently, 'get your leaf out, spin around three times and run.'

No sooner had they done this than they disappeared just as the witch had finished her curse and a flash of blue light made a direct hit on a toadstool where they had been.

True to the witch's threat, the toadstool

had turned into a dinner plate.

Rewsin and Longstint hid behind a clump of moss and watched the witch; she was enraged.

'When I catch you I will not only put a curse on you, I'll put a curse on your next door neighbour, and your next door neighbour's budgerigar!' she screamed.

Just then, the unfortunate Duffy caught the witch's eye. 'Ah,' she said, walking toward the little bird's lifeless body, 'this looks like it might make a tasty Scrunnock pie for me supper.'

'Oh no!' thought Longstint, then shouted, 'We are over here, ugly witch,' then started running.

The witch turned her attention away from Duffy and started toward Longstint's voice.

The Willigrews started to run around in circles, shouting as they went, in order to confuse the witch.

'We're over here,' they said. Then 'No we're not, we're over there.' The witch was so confused she ran around in circles firing blue flashes in different directions.

Before long, the forest floor was covered in dinner plates and various other items of crockery.

Then, horror of horrors the witch turned and looked straight at the little green twosome, 'GOTCHA!' she squealed in delight.

The turnip leaves had stopped working and the Willigrews were now visible again.

The witch started her chant again, 'Lumpkin, dumpkin, waddling goose.'

Longstint turned to Rewsin and said defiantly, 'I don't know about you old pal, but I'm not at the right stage in my life to become part of a dinner service, let's get her.'

With that, they ran toward the startled witch and grabbing a leg each, they tipped her over.

Longstint took her broomstick and threw it into the bushes. The witch shouted 'Not me broomstick. I can't carry on without me broomstick.'

When she ran into the bushes to retrieve it the Willigrews picked Duffy up and ran as fast as they could away from the witch and into the distance.

When they felt they were safe from the witches clutches, they sat down on the side of the path and lay Duffy on a pile of soft moss.

Rewsin stroked Duffy's little feathery head.

'Poor little Duffy,' he cried. 'So brave, you gave your life to save ours and now we can't help you.'

Longstint knelt beside them, wiped a tear from his eye and said, 'Goodbye little Duffy, faithful friend, we shall miss you.'

Just then the Scrunnock gave a little twitch, then a medium sized twitch, then a big twitch, then, to the delight of the Willigrews, said, 'I should hope you would miss me. How would you find your way without my superior avian navigational skills, your flying satnav?'

Rewsin and Longstint were so relieved and happy, that they did the Willigrew dance, hopping about on one leg and flicking their earlobes with their index fingers.

After Duffy had rested for a while, the little troupe carried on up the mountain. They left the Mossy Forest and the witch behind them and headed for the next encounter.

They didn't have to wait long.

'What's that up ahead?' asked Rewsin, 'it looks like a field of giant toadstools.'

Sure enough, before them was a wonderful sight, what must have been thousands of toadstools. Red ones with white spots, white ones with red spots, yellow ones with no spots and ones that looked a bit like they were once invisible!

'Wow!' exclaimed Duffy, 'it looks like a fungi forest, let's explore.'

On entering the forest, they were greeted by a strong smell of mushrooms, then a soft voice came from on top of a toadstool.

'Welcome friends, to my forest. I am Chloe the kindly fairy, I am so delighted to meet you.'

The fairy floated down from the toadstool and landed softly on the ground before the Willigrews.

She was very beautiful, dressed in green lace with sparkly green wings, which glittered and glistened. In her hair, she wore three bright shiny, golden flowers.

She took Longstint's breath away (but soon gave it back as she thought he might need it).

'Oh I do love visitors,' said the fairy, 'you must stay and have some refreshment. We have fairy cakes, but they are not made from real fairies.'

'Yummo,' said Longstint, 'I am partial to a nice bit of cake.'

'Then you shall have as many as your little green tummy can hold,' promised the fairy.

Fairy Chloe then sprinkled some green fairy dust onto the ground and a large pile of cakes, in every colour of the rainbow, appeared as if by magic (well, I suppose it was magic, but you know what I mean).

Rewsin and Longstint got stuck in and Duffy pecking away at the delicious cakes said, 'Crumbs, I do love crumbs. My favourite bit is the topping, that's the icing on the cake.'

'Oops, I almost forgot,' said Rewsin, handing Chloe the recipe that Princess Tabitha had given him. 'And the Princess sends her royal regards.'

'Jumbly Dumplings, how delightful. Tabs is such a thoughtful person.' said Chloe scanning the ingredients. 'I will have to go shopping tomorrow to buy some pomegranate flour and jangleberry juice.'

Having eaten their fill, the trio thanked Fairy Chloe and said they would get going again.

'But, before you go, allow me to give you all a gift,' beamed Chloe. 'I know, I will turn your noses back to their normal colour.' She sprinkled fairy dust on the two noses and the one beak and all was well in the nose department.

'What a relief,' sighed Duffy. 'Thank you so much, we will always remember you as a kind fairy, with a heart of gold and wings of green and very nice shoes.'

Just then, he paused, 'I'm waffling again, aren't I?'

Both the Willigrews and Chloe nodded knowingly, and then had a group chuckle.

Just as they were leaving, Chloe gave them each some fairy dust in small paper bags.

She explained that all they had to do was sprinkle it on and make a wish. Warning them to use it wisely, she waved to them as they trundled off on their way.

They spent the next few metres just climbing past fairly uninteresting sights.

Rewsin thought he saw a fierce triceratops hiding behind a tree, but it turned out to be just a rather large bandicoot, wearing a reasonably fashionable baseball cap and playing a violin, so nothing unusual.

However, they all saw the next thing. The dark blurry thing was back. It dashed across their path, turned to look at them and disappeared around a corner.

What they saw made them shiver with fright. It had dark, dark green scaly skin, with vivid red eyes and uneven fangs protruding from its wet slavering mouth!

Duffy spoke, with a quivering voice, 'I really hope I'm wrong, but I remember when I was a chick my mum told me about such a creature.'

She called it the Beast of the Moonlight Shadow, and told me to avoid it at all costs.

'Always remember,' she told me, 'if you see this evil monster, fly away as fast as your wings will take you.'

'Scary, or what?' said Longstint, trying to sound brave.

'Anyway, Duffy,' asked Rewsin, 'why didn't you do what your mum said, and fly away?'

'Well, my mum also said that you should never let your friends down.' replied Duffy.

They were all a little more watchful as they continued their trek up the mountain.

They were about half way up now and the going was easy, not too steep, with few obstacles.

They did meet a group of orange spiders, however, who shared a cup of chickweed tea with them and spoke about politics and philosophy in the world of the spider, which was sort of interesting, but uneventful, so they carried on up the mountain.

Duffy, having flown ahead, came whizzing back and breathlessly told the Willigrews there was a small crowd further along the track.

He explained that they looked like toy soldiers. They were heavily armed and their legs were quite big as well.

Rewsin and Longstint walked on for a while until eventually they came upon the group of soldiers. They approached, not knowing what sort of reception they would get.

However, they soon found out as a gun was pointed in their direction.

'Put your hands on your heads, keep still, and don't move a muscle, or we'll fire,' barked the first soldier.

The Willigrews followed the orders. The soldier walked over to them and prodded Rewsin in the chest with his rifle.

We are the prison guards and you've got to come with us,' he ordered.

They were taken to a building at the side of the track, where a large barred door was opened and they were pushed inside.

To the Willigrews dismay, the guard told them that they were to be imprisoned forever, with no chance of release.

'But, we have done nothing wrong,' protested Rewsin, 'why are we being punished?'

'I don't know really, but I'll think of something, now be quiet,' replied the guard, with a sneer.

One of the other guards then shouted, 'They're too green.'

'That's it,' said the first guard, 'that's your crime, you're too green.' He then walked away, leaving the Willigrews locked up.

'I don't like his attitude,' complained Longstint, 'he's being greenist.'

As they sat, trying to think of a plan, there was a movement at the back of the prison followed by a voice that said, wearily, 'You'll never escape, we've all been here for years, and we've tried everything.'

Rewsin turned, and was astonished to see six figures walking towards him. These were not just any old figures (no, they were not Marks and Spencer's figures) but green figures.

They were Willigrews! They turned out to be the missing six whose names were on the monument.

There, before them, stood Vodrabo, Enog, Dornig, Colmanda, Benmanda and Nostrilgaw, looking a bit thin but happy to see their friends.

All the Willigrews hugged one another. The six looked very weak and thin, and explained that they were only given one bowl of grass soup a day.

Longstint happened to have a few chickweed biscuits in his bag, so handed them around. These were gratefully scoffed down, followed by six loud burps and six 'beg pardons'.

Rewsin assured the others that he would think of a plan to get them all out and back home to Willigrew, but just needed a bit of time to think.

They all sat in a circle, as Willigrews do, and talked about what had been happening back home, and all the adventures and gossip.

It was dark outside by now and Rewsin still hadn't come up with a plan.

Just then there was flapping followed by a soft tweeting sound, and, through the prison bars came little Duffy Scrunnock.

'Quickly,' he said, 'there was only one guard on duty and I sent him to sleep with my fairy dust in a small paper bag. Remember, all you have to do is sprinkle it and make a wish.'

'OK,' said Longstint, and sprinkled his fairy dust in the small paper bag, on the cell door, 'I wish this door would open.'

They waited just a few moments, then the door swung open and all the Willigrews quietly filed out.

'This way,' whispered Duffy, 'there's an escape route through the tall grass.'

They all followed the little bird, keeping as quiet as they could, until they reached safety.

Once they were out of earshot they all did the Willigrew dance again, they were feeling so happy. Duffy flew around in circles above their heads singing a merry tune.

The problem for Rewsin and Longstint now, was whether to complete their mission to get to the top of the Might Stump, or to accompany the other Willigrews back to their homes.

After much discussion, drinking of chickweed tea, walking backwards and forwards and pointing at each other's feet, they decided to carry on upward.

In fact, they were all in the mood for adventure after their escape from the prison and felt ready for whatever lay ahead.

So the eight Willigrews and one bird set off toward the summit.

'Let's do the hopping song.' suggested Nostrilgaw.

The little band moved off in a row, happily hopping and singing, bumping into each other, falling over and getting up again, then falling over again.

Let's all hop, and never stop,
Let's all hop, till we reach the top,
Cos when you're hopping,
There's no time for stopping,
So let's all hop and never stop.

Duffy landed on the ground and joined in with the hopping, which made the Willigrews laugh and cheer.

Then, just as they were getting a bit exhausted, they noticed that the sky had turned dark and gloomy.

Rewsin said that he didn't like the look of this, and that it might be another storm, but just as they were preparing to run for cover they looked up.

What they saw, in the sky above them, made them all shake with fear. The sight was so fearsome that even Longstint was a bit frightened.

A gigantic dragon was hovering above them, snorting fire and a little bit of snot, which sprayed the Willigrews, from its huge nostrils.

Then the dragon let out a loud, ear-splitting scream. 'Ooohlah,' it went, making the ground shake.

'You have dared to enter the dragon's realm,' roared the awesome monster. 'You are all doomed to be burnt to a crisp. I would have done it already, but I like to do a bit of scary shouting first.'

The Willigrews and Duffy were just becoming resigned to their grizzly fate when Longstint (who else?) spoke.

'I must admit, old dragony thing, I am very impressed with your scary shouting. I've heard lots of scary shouting in my life, but yours is excellent. I would go as far as to say that your scary shouting is second to none.'

'Have you ever thought of entering yourself into the Scary Shouting World Cup, I'm sure you would win.'

The dragon looked down at Longstint and, with a confused, cross-eyed look on his horrible face, said 'Do you really think so? I do practise a lot, in my spare time, that's probably why

I'm so good.'

Longstint continued, 'and that flame-throwing thing you do is even better. Would you show us again?'

'Oh, all right then,' replied the dragon, 'but I will burn you to a crisp when I've finished.'

The dragon didn't disappoint Longstint, the flames (and snot) that came from its nose lit up the sky, burning down trees and bushes and making the ground smoke.

'Quickly,' urged Longstint to the others, 'clap and cheer.'

Not quite knowing why, the others did what Longstint said, and cheered, clapped, stamped their feet and shouted, 'Respect, respect for the Snot Dragon,' encouraging the dragon to fire out more flame and smoke.

'More, more,' shouted the Willigrews.

However, then, the dragon turned its attention to the cheering group and aimed its angry fire at them.

The large flame travelled straight at our little heroes, but to their amazing astonishment, it didn't reach them, although they were covered in snot.

'Drat,' cursed the dragon, looking a bit embarrassed, 'I've run out of fire. It will take me ages to charge up my nostrils again.'

'I say you little green chaps, you wouldn't mind hanging around for a couple of days while I charge up my nostrils, would you? I was rather looking forward to burning you to a crisp.'

'Thanks for the offer, mate, but I think we'll pass on that,' answered Rewsin.

'Brilliant,' shouted Longstint, gleefully, 'my plan worked, now let's leg it.'

With that, the Willigrews ran toward the summit as fast as their little green furry legs would carry them.

The dragon sat on the ground, looking very miserable, and watched them go, wondering how he was silly enough to fall for Longstint's cunning trick.

It didn't take the Willigrews long to reach the top of the stump. Duffy was first, and shouted to the others to hurry up, because the view was spectacular.

When they caught up, they could only agree, they could see for miles and miles across the countryside.

There was, however, one higher place before they reached the absolute top, a small stump of wood. Everyone agreed that, because of his quick thinking and calmness under pressure, Longstint should take the last step.

'Thank you all,' said Longstint, humbly.

As he stepped onto the small stump he said, 'This is one small step for a Willigrew, but a giant leap for Willigrewkind!'

The others cheered and shouted 'Longstint, Longstint, you' the man, you' the man!'

After eating a supper of chickweed biscuits and tea, they all settled down for the night to get some serious kip.

As the food was being shared among eight now, they decided to try to make it last until they returned home, so they ate it slowly to make it last longer.

The Willigrews awoke in the morning to the usual sound of Duffy and his morning chorus. 'Sorry about the noise,' he said, 'it's my job.'

Rewsin suggested that they try a different route down the Stump, to try to avoid some of the nasties that they encountered on the way up, and everyone agreed.

Duffy led the way, as usual, and the others trundled along behind him.

Nothing much happened for a while, until they came upon another sign, which read:

HERE THERE BE MORE LOBECHOMPERS, CLOSELY RELATED TO THE OTHER LOBECHOMPERS ON THE MAIN PATH

Just as Longstint was about to warn everyone to cover their earlobes, Benmanda gave out a loud squeal. 'Ow, it's got my lobe.'

Hanging from Benmanda's ear was what looked like a snail with a semi-detached shell and metallic wings. It made horrible slurpy munching noises, much to Benmanda's horror.

'Quick, get it off me,' she cried, 'it really hurts quite a lot.'

The others couldn't hear her cries because they had their ears covered, but they could see what was happening. There were Lobechompers everywhere, hundreds of them, circling around above the Willigrews' heads.

Longstint ran over to Benmanda and tried to pull the Lobechomper off, but it was stuck fast. He was alarmed to see that Benmanda's ear was bleeding quite badly.

However, as he had to uncover his own ears, a Lobechomper clamped itself to him.

'Yow, ooh, ouch.' he squealed.

The Lobechompers were about to move in on the others, when, suddenly, as if out of nowhere, a green flash appeared.

It was Chloe the fairy, coming to the rescue. She carried a magic wand, and pointed it at the Lobechomper attached to Benmanda's ear.

'Zap,' she shouted, as a bolt of green light struck the creature, which flew into the air, but not before one final chomp.

After doing the same for Longstint she chased all the other Lobechompers off by waving her wand in their direction.

Chloe apologised for having to make the 'Zap' sound herself because the Autozap feature on her wand was not working properly.

'I must look for that wand insurance policy

I took out,' she said.

Longstint and Rewsin were delighted to see Chloe again, and thanked her for coming to their aid.

'I was looking for you, in fact,' she said, 'I thought you might like some cake for your journey home. It's a new recipe I obtained from the New Recipe Fairy and it's called 'lemon right way up cake'. I do hope you like it.'

'I'm sure we will,' replied Longstint licking his lips.

'Yummo,' agreed Duffy, who was sitting on Chloe's shoulder.

After putting some magicky ointment on Benmanda's and Longstint's ears, Chloe said her goodbyes, and, amid much waving and blowing of kisses and flying around in circles, she flew off into the distance, leaving a trail of green sparkliness behind her.

The Willigrews and Duffy were missing their homes now and made their minds up to head down the Stump as soon as possible.

They didn't come across any more problems until they were almost out of the boodad trees at the foot of the Stump.

Spirits were high as the happy band walked through the forest, when suddenly

Duffy gave out a loud chirp.

Looking up the Willigrews saw that a large bird had Duffy in its talons, and was carrying him off.

'That must be the Harrow Spawk he told us about,' groaned Rewsin. 'Poor Duffy, he's doomed.'

'Not if I can help it,' said a deep voice from behind a tree (it might have been a voice from behind a deep tree). 'I will save your feathery friend.'

It was, to the Willigrews' amazement, unmistakably, The Beast of the Moonlight Shadow.

It stared up at the birds, which were now quite high in the sky, and, from his eyes, produced a stream of golden light, which surrounded the Harrow Spawk.

A loud squawking noise came from the Harrow Spawk, and it released little Duffy, who came tumbling down towards the ground. Just as he was about to crash land, the Beast caught him and gently placed him on the ground.

'There, there,' said the Beast reassuringly.

'Where, where,' replied Duffy, when he saw who had saved him.

'Aren't you supposed to be an evil monster?' enquired Rewsin, 'and haven't you been following us?'

The Beast spoke, 'Well, I don't blame you for thinking that, but that's just my reputation. You see, I have been watching over you to make sure you were safe. I am so sorry if I frightened you, but I hide away as much as possible, especially during the day, because I am so terribly ugly.'

'You see I never wanted to be a beast when I was a child. I wanted to work in a 'call centre'.'

Longstint wanted to say, 'Well you're no oil

painting mate', but he, like the others, began to feel a bit sorry for the Beast, and said instead, 'You're not ugly at all, just different.'

Benmanda went even further by saying, 'In fact, I think you are quite handsome in a sort of gruesome way. A nice hair wash and a visit to the dentist to have your fangs polished, and you could become quite the dashing Beast.'

'Just you go and visit Trudey Jellegerk, the fashion advisor. She'll sort you out.' She advised, handing over Trudey's business card.

'Do you really think so?' asked the Beast, who was warming to the Willigrews.

'You have just proven to us that you are good,' explained Rewsin, 'even the most beautiful creature becomes ugly if it is badly evil. You see, good is beautiful and evil is ugly, whatever it looks like.'

Before too long the Beast was sitting down and sharing the lemon cake. Well, I say sharing, because he ate the whole thing in one huge gulp.

However, the Willigrews didn't mind, and gave him a nice cup of chickweed tea to wash it down with.

'Wow, that was totally yumsome,' said the Beast, licking one of his fangs. 'Thank you very much.'

Enog was curious, and asked the Beast what its real name was.

'I'd almost forgotten,' he replied, 'but I used to be called Cedric by my parents.'

'Well, Cedric is a lovely name and not a name for a Beast at all. We shall all call you Cedric from this moment onwards,' enthused Benmanda.

'So are we to call him The Cedric of The Moonlight Shadow now?' asked Duffy, who was sitting on Cedric's head, looking for insects.

The others laughed and said, all together, 'No, just Cedric.'

A happy, more confident Cedric waved farewell to the Willigrews and headed out to find Trudey Jellegerk to arrange a makeover.

'Well, that was a surprise.' said Rewsin as the little band headed home, on the last leg of their journey, and the others agreed.

Duffy flew on ahead, to tell the inhabitants of Willigrew that their heroes were on the way home.

The rest of the trip was quite uneventful and, eventually, the little group of travellers arrived, tired and hungry, in Willigrew.

Bronglay and Yill had arranged a huge reception for the homecoming, with large colourful banners, music, dancing, lots of silliness and plenty of food.

Before the festivities started, Bronglay gave a speech to the assembled crowd.

'Fellow Willigrews, I would like you to join me in welcoming our brave heroes home.'

'They have not only conquered The Mighty Stump of Doom, but have also rescued the long lost Willigrews who have been missing for so long. We Willigrews are naturally curious and, despite the dangers, we will always look for new experiences and adventures, but it is always nice to come home to the safety of the village.'

Realising that he was 'going on a bit' and that some of the crowd had nodded off, Bronglay wound up his speech (put it on the ground, where it went around in little circles) by thanking Duffy Scrunnock, who, at some risk to his own life, had assisted the Willigrews in their adventure.

'I would like to invite Duffy to live with us in our village and be our number one feathered friend,' he said, finally.

The audience cheered and did the

Willigrew national dance, and Duffy flew around in circles, twitching and chirping in agreement.

The End

THE WILLIGREWS AND THE
MYSTERIOUS EGG

It was wintertime in Willigrew, and the snow lay deeply on the ground around the village.

The chickweed beds were buried under deep snow, so the Willigrews could not tend the fields; they had to rely on the food they had stored up in the autumn. This meant that our little green friends did not have much to do with their time.

Lots of snowwilligrews had been built, and everyone had enjoyed the snowball fights, but Longstint was feeling a bit bored, so decided to take a walk in the fields for a while.

He wandered about, leaving footprints in the snow, and thought about little things like ants and beetles and some big things like big ants and big beetles.

He stopped, however, when, as he passed a jangleberry bush, he saw something a bit strange. Right in the middle of the bush was a large purple egg.

'That's an egg,' he said to himself, 'and it's purple, what's a purple egg doing there in the middle of winter?'

Worried that whatever was inside the egg

would freeze in the snow, he found a few fallen branches and draped them over the egg to keep it warm.

'What to do? What to do?' he thought, 'Bronglay, I'd better tell Bronglay, he'll know what to do.'

With that, Longstint started back to the village, half running, half walking (his right half was running, and his left half was walking).

He soon arrived outside Bronglay's house and knocked on the door, which Yill opened. She welcomed him in, saying, 'Come in Longstint, out of the cold, there is some tea on the go.'

'Sorry, Yill, I haven't time to stop. I need to speak with Bronglay straight away please,' he replied breathlessly.

Bronglay came into the hall and asked Longstint what the urgency was.

Longstint explained about the egg and he and Bronglay left immediately to investigate.

'Here it is,' said Longstint, as they approached the jangleberry bush, pointing in its direction.

Bronglay looked at the egg very closely, and then touched it. 'It's still warm,' he said, 'we must get it back to Willigrew as soon as possible.'

Very gently, he picked it up and, cradling it in his arms, took it back to his house.

When they got back, Krowfin was there, having heard about the egg.

'Dear me, this is a turn up and no mistake,' said Krowfin. 'I wonder what's inside, I hope it's nothing dangerous, I'm not all that keen on dangerous things coming out of eggs.'

'Well, whatever it is, it will only be a baby, and babies aren't normally dangerous, even the babies of dangerous things,' argued Yill.

'First things first,' said Bronglay, 'we will need to put it somewhere warm and safe until it hatches.'

'And I've got just the thing,' an excited Krowfin said. 'What about the propagator that we use to germinate our chickweed seeds, perfect or what?'

Everyone agreed and Krowfin soon returned with the propagator, which was large enough to take the egg. It had a clear lid to keep the egg safe, and was heated. He put it on the kitchen table.

Yill placed the egg inside, and Krowfin put the lid on. Then they all stood around and stared at the shiny purple object.

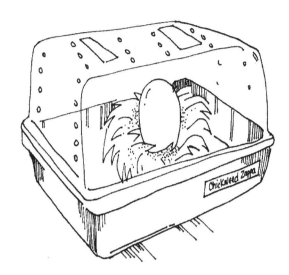

After a few minutes of staring, the Willigrews looked at each other and smiled.

'Staring at it will not make it hatch, will it?' said Yill.

'You are right, my little green banana. I think we should take it in turns to watch the egg until it hatches,' suggested Bronglay.

'Me first, please, me first, thank you, please very much,' cried Krowfin jumping up and down.

How could the others refuse? Therefore, everybody else went about their business of doing nothing and Krowfin sat down at the table and set about his watching duties.

After about ten minutes of watching, Krowfin started to get a bit impatient.

'I've been sitting here for about ten million years, when is something going to happen?' he asked himself.

No sooner had he said this when he thought he heard something. A deep gurgling sound was coming from the egg. The sound was a sort of cross between a frog croaking and a tall gentleman with a sore throat.

Krowfin became very excited and called for everyone to come and listen.

'Quickly, everyone come and listen, the egg made a noise, a gentleman frog croaking, sort of thing. Hurry, it might be hatching!' he shrieked.

The others soon arrived, now joined by Rewsin and Father, and gathered around the table to listen. The egg, however, was silent.

'Are you sure it isn't your tummy rumbling?' asked Yill.

'I don't think it's my tummy,' replied Krowfin, 'it was definitely a gurgle.'

'A gurgle?' asked Longstint, looking at Bronglay. 'What is a gurgle, and what does a gurgle look like. I've never heard of such a thing. Do gurgles lay eggs then?'

Everybody laughed, except the egg, which gurgled again, much to Krowfin's relief. He was beginning to think it *was* his rumbly tum after all.

'You were spot on Krowfers old chap,' said Bronglay. 'That was definitely a gurgle, but not just any old gurgle, that was a classic mysterious egg type gurgle.'

Whatever was inside the egg must have gone to sleep, because there were no more sounds for several hours. By which time Father was on duty watch.

Yill had brought in some chickweed tea and biscuits and she and Father sat together to wait for some sign of life from the propagator.

'This egg business is all a bit strange Father, I wonder where it came from, it seemed to come out of nowhere,' asked Yill.

'I haven't a clue Mum,' replied Father, 'but it's funny you should say that, because there is something I have always wondered about. Where *is* nowhere?

'I'm glad you asked. You see, I have a theory about that,' Yill explained. 'I don't think 'nowhere' exists! If you were to look for 'nowhere', you would never find it, because, when you get to nowhere it immediately becomes somewhere, if you see what I mean. If you are there it must be somewhere, so 'nowhere' does not exist.'

Father pondered Yill's theory for a while but, before he could answer her, another sound came from the propagator.

There was the usual gurgle, but this time the usual gurgle was followed by an unusual loud 'crack'.

'I think it's about to hatch out,' said Father excitedly. 'I'll get the others.'

Father ran off in a panic and did a bit of a Krowfin, instead of leaving by the back door, he ran into a cupboard.

When he came out of the cupboard, looking a bit embarrassed he said, 'I just thought I would check the cupboard before I went, everything seems all right in there.'

Yill smiled then turned her attention back to the egg.

It was not long before a crowd had gathered around the propagator.

Rewsin, munching on a chickweed biscuit, asked, 'Do you think it will hatch soon, I am really excited?'

Yill rebuked him gently, by saying, 'Don't eat with your mouth full my little greengage.'

This confused Rewsin, but he didn't argue, just kept munching.

Then it happened. The crack in the egg grew wider and as the shell fell away. A shape emerged, covered in wet slime.

As Bronglay removed the propagator lid, a strange looking being emerged. It was small, even to the Willigrews, and round and bald, like a ball.

It had neither arms nor legs, just piercing black eyes, two flat nostrils and a black tube shaped mouth, which stuck out from its face, quite a long way.

It then bounced out of the propagator onto the table, shook itself very vigorously and sprayed wet gooey slime over the Willigrews!

'Errgh, gross,' complained Longstint, wiping the slime from his face.

Before anyone could agree, the creature, to the amazement of all, spoke!

'Hello, everyone, my name is Georgie, and I have just hatched out from my egg. It was really hot in there. Any chance of a drink of water, I'm gasping.'

As Yill gave Georgie a glass of water, she asked, 'How did you learn to speak so soon?'

'Don't ask me,' replied Georgie, 'I have always been able to speak. I only know one thing, and that is I must find the other egg, I need to find Georgette.'

'Another egg?' gasped Yill, 'you mean there's another egg?'

'Georgie says yes,' Georgie replied. 'Will you help Georgie find it?'

The Willigrews, of course agreed to help search for the egg. Apart from wanting to help their new friend, they were, understandably, very curious.

Outside it had started snowing again, so, worried that the egg might be covered, the Willigrews searched with some urgency. (Zamborina had found the urgency under a tree and thought it might come in handy when searching for something).

'You go ahead behind me,' said Krowfin, 'and look out for another jangleberry bush, that's where the other egg was.'

The group of searchers trudged through the snow, followed by Georgie who bounced along beside them, singing a little song:

I love to bounce,
Bouncing is fun,
If I had legs,
I would not run
I would bounce all the time,
Bounce on my bum,
And if it got cold,
I would bounce on my tum,
Cos bouncing is fun.

Of course, the Willigrews could not resist joining in and, before long, they were all bouncing along with Georgie, making big footprints in the crispy snow and singing the song.

Just then, Longstint shouted, 'Egg alert, egg alert, I have found the egg, it's over here.'

Georgie was first on the scene, and started

to bounce around in little circles saying, 'Georgie says Georgie likes Longstint. Longstint found the egg.' He then let out a low humming whistley sound from his tubey mouth, which vibrated at the end, like a balloon deflating, and to everyone's surprise, the egg rose, unaided, into the air and floated toward Georgie.

Georgie then made his way back to Bronglay's house with the egg floating behind him.

When they got back, Bronglay put the second egg into the propagator and they all waited in anticipation for it to hatch.

Eventually, after several cups of tea and quite a few biscuits, there were signs of life, as the usual gurgling and cracking produced another creature, not unlike Georgie, from the egg.

The Willigrews managed to avoid the slime this time by standing well back from the shaking Georgette. When she was dry, Georgie bounced onto the table and snuggled up close to her and they both made little squeaking noises.

'This everybody,' announced Georgie, 'is Georgette. Georgie says have you ever seen a lovelier Georgette in your lives?'

'I agree,' Krowfin replied, nodding his head, 'as Georgettes go, she is very lovely. In fact I would go as far as to say that, of all the Georgettes I have met, she is the loveliest.'

'Georgette says thank you kind sir,' said Georgette, fluttering her eyelids.

After all the excitement had died down and most of the Willigrews had gone home, Bronglay and Yill sat down with their new friends and tried to find out a bit more about them.

Georgette explained that they were Mardronians from a planet called Byclipss, in the galaxy of Goodlon.

Their planet had come under attack from creatures called the Yippets.

'We had no defence against them,' said Georgie tearfully. 'They carried tortoise guns on their heads, which fired rays of light, which made our people disappear and never return.

Our leader, Squarthur, decided, in desperation, to put us in the eggs and fire us into outer space in the hope that we might land safely on another planet.

I fear that the rest of our race has perished at the hands of the Yippets'.

'That is so sad,' said Yill, stroking Georgette's head, 'but you are safe now in Willigrew, we will look after you.'

'There is one thing that worries me about the Yippets,' said Georgie. 'They have sworn to destroy every last inhabitant of our planet, and they may come looking for us. We do not want to put your tribe in danger, as you have been so kind to us.'

'Willigrews,' announced Bronglay, looking very serious, 'will protect their friends, whatever the cost and whatever the danger. We'll deal with these Yippets if and when they come, or die trying.'

Feeling reassured by Bronglay's words the Mardronians, snuggled down in the propagator and went to sleep.

During the night, Yill awoke when she heard crying coming from the kitchen. When she looked in, she saw Georgette in floods of tears.

'Whatever can be wrong?' she asked.

'I miss my family, and my planet,' Georgette sobbed 'I will never see them again.'

Yill was about say 'chin up', but realised that Georgette didn't have one (chin that is).

Therefore, she tried to console her by

patting her on the head, but stopped when she started to bounce up and down nearly bouncing off the table.

That having failed Yill said 'Don't worry little one, we will find a way to sort things out, and, don't forget, you have lots of friends in Willigrew. We will never let you down.'

With that, feeling a little happier, Georgette went back to sleep.

The next morning, after a breakfast of chickweed porridge and a nice cup of tea (the tea was nice and so was the cup), Bronglay called a meeting in the Meeting Hall, which is where the Willigrews held all their meetings (which, I suppose, was why it was called the Meeting Hall).

At the meeting, Bronglay stood on the stage to address the meeting, but he forgot their postcode, so decided instead, to speak to them.

'Welcome Willigrews,' he began. 'First of all I would like to welcome our new friends, Georgie and Georgette. They are in great need of our help, as they have had to escape from their home planet Byclipss. I know you will all make them welcome and not pat them on the head, as they are prone to a bit of bouncing.'

He then explained about the Yippets and that everyone should look out for anything unusual, like spacecraft landing or strange footprints in the snow.

Bronglay finished by saying, 'Let us not forget that our guests are representing the Mardronian nation and we must treat them as we do each other. Thank you all for coming, I will see you later, or earlier, whichever comes first.'

After a few days, the Mardronians had met all the Willigrews and seemed to be settling in all right. The snow was still falling and getting deeper by the minute.

Not much happened for a while, until, one night, Krowfin, who was on sky watch, banged loudly on Bronglay's door. Bronglay opened the door to a slightly agitated Krowfin.

'Quickly, Bronglay, come and look,' he cried, pointing to the sky, 'strange lights. Look!'

Bronglay looked up and what he saw sent a chill through most of his body (his left foot seemed to be coping all right).

Orange lights in the sky, there must have been about a dozen of them. Was this an invasion? Had the Yippets come looking for

Georgie and Georgette?

The lights then disappeared behind some trees in the distance.

'This may be what we were dreading,' warned Bronglay. 'We must take a look to see where they landed.'

'Why don't we ask Duffy to go? Asked Krowfin.

I think it only fair to explain that Duffy Scrunnock is a small bird that befriended the Willigrews in another story, '*The Willigrews and The Mighty Stump of Doom*'.

This twitchy little character now lives in Willigrew with his new friends and only goes back to his own family for important meetings and feasts.

'Good thinking Krowfers old chap,' replied Bronglay, 'let's find him.'

They soon found Duffy, roosting for the night, in a tree. His head tucked under his wing.

'Wake up Duffy,' urged Bronglay, 'we need your assistance.'

'What,' exclaimed a startled Duffy, 'it can't be morning already? It's not very light yet.'

'Don't, whatever you do, start your morning chorus, or you will wake the whole village,'

Bronglay added.

'Cor, that's a relief,' said Duffy, 'that always gives me such a headache. I take it that you need my avian expertise?'

Krowfin explained about the lights in the sky and asked Duffy to fly over to take a look. In addition, to be careful as this mission could be dangerous.

Duffy set off straight away, flying upwards until he disappeared behind the trees and out of sight.

Bronglay and Krowfin decided to go back to Bronglay's house and have some breakfast.

When they got there, Bronglay prepared a pot of chickweed tea and a couple of bowls of Chickweed flakes. They both washed their hands and dried them thoroughly, which is what the Willigrews always did to avoid diseases and other nasty things.

You see there had been quite a lot of sneezing in the village lately, and, if you read The Willigrews and the Big Sneeze, you will know what a problem that caused. Therefore, Bronglay posted a sign on the notice board at the Meeting Hall, telling everyone to sneeze into a tissue and put it straight into a bin.

A couple of hours passed before Duffy

returned. Yill spotted him flying over the trees and watched him until he landed on the ground at her feet.

'That was a bit hairy,' said Duffy, twitching, as usual.

'Dangerous journey?' asked Yill.

'No,' Duffy replied, 'I've just seen a long-haired yelpsnapper sitting in a treetop. It was really hairy, even for a long-haired yelpsnapper.'

By now, several other Willigrews and the two Mardronians had gathered around Duffy, curious to find out what he had seen.

'What have you seen?' they all asked together (See I told you so).

'It doesn't look good,' Duffy began. 'Some strange metallic craft have landed on the other side of the forest. There must be about twenty of them. I sat watching for a while until a door on one of them opened and a spidery looking creature with four legs came out.'

'On its back, it carried what looked like a tortoise. Several others followed it out and when other doors started to open, I decided to take a closer look.'

'However, as I landed on a low branch near them, they must have spotted me and one of them fired some sort of light ray from the tortoise on its back. I decided it was too dangerous to hang about, so I flew back here to report my findings.'

'Sounds like the Yippets have come looking for Georgie and Georgette,' said Bronglay, looking knowingly at Krowfin. 'I think we should call a meeting straightaway.'

Just then, Rewsin pointed toward Duffy and exclaimed, 'Where has your left wing gone?'

Duffy looked down and, sure enough, his left wing had disappeared.

'Eek!' he cried. 'It's gone, but I can still feel it. It has become invisible.'

'Oh no!' squealed a terrified Georgette, the Yippet must have hit you with a light ray.'

'Don't worry, my little bouncy friend,' said Duffy, reassuringly, 'it doesn't hurt, although I am not as symmetrical as I was, and I was very proud of my symmetry. We birds take great pride in being symmetrical.'

Longstint, Rewsin and Dora Dingbat volunteered to stand guard on the village border, in case the Yippets appeared without warning. The rest went back to the Meeting Hall.

Bronglay was first to speak, saying, 'Fellow Willigrews, it looks as though our village is about to be attacked by unfriendly creatures from another planet. This could be the greatest threat we have ever faced, but I know you will defend Willigrew bravely and prevent the Yippets from harming our Mardronian guests. Now I would like you all to put on your thinking caps and see if you can come up with some ideas.'

Everyone proceeded to put on their thinking caps, which were little pointy numbers in a nice shade of turquoise. Everyone, that is, except Repscar, who had forgotten his, so he had to draw a picture of it and stick to his forehead.

In fact, it was Repscar, who came up with the first idea. 'Why don't we just run away and come back when the Yippets have gone? I don't want to disappear. I won't know where I am. What if I wake up and find I'm not there?'

The others, knowing that Repscar was a bit of a wimp, laughed at his suggestion. Krowfin said that Willigrews never run away, although they might make the odd strategic withdrawal.

Bronglay, as understanding as ever, reassured Repscar, by saying that he wouldn't be in any danger.

'It's all right Repscar,' added Longstint, 'you can hide behind me.'

'Cheers mate,' said a relieved Repscar.

The next idea was a bit more sensible and came from Father, who suggested that they all hold up mirrors, to reflect the light rays back at the Yippets, in the hope that it would make them disappear.

'Great idea,' said Krowfin, 'although I see one big snag. Where are we going to find enough mirrors for everyone?'

Somebody suggested using shiny vegetables, but the others did not take that seriously.

Bronglay could see no other solution to the problem so asked everyone who owned a mirror to bring it to the Meeting Hall as soon as possible.

'The Willigrews who don't have mirrors will just have to stand behind the ones who do,' he suggested.

After much dashing about, running up and down and bumping into each other, all the Willigrews arrived back at the Meeting Hall.

Those with mirrors held them up and those without mirrors didn't. Although one held up a shiny courgette, still thinking this was a good idea.

Bronglay stood on the stage, and, when everyone had quietened down, he said. 'OK, everyone this is the plan.'

'We plan to use mirrors to reflect the laser beams back at the Yippets, so making them disappear instead. I know this idea seems a bit silly and may not work, but it's all anyone could think of at the time. We will assemble on the edge of the village by the chickweed beds at midnight.'

'Just one more thing, as you know, it is still snowing outside so wrap up warm and take a flask of tea with you. Father has made a batch of jangleberry jam sandwiches, so nobody should go hungry. See you all at midnight and good luck little Willigrews.'

Just before midnight, Bronglay and Yill joined up with Dora, Rewsin and Longstint at the edge of the village. They had nothing to report, as everything had been quiet, with no sign of the Yippets.

Pretty soon, a large crowd had gathered and Bronglay sorted them into ranks. The ones with mirrors were to stand at the front and those without were to stand behind them.

As they sat and waited, Longstint turned to Yill and asked, 'Do you think it is possible to find something that isn't lost?'

Yill replied, looking a bit puzzled, 'Mmm. That is a strange question. What made you think of that at this present moment in time?'

'Well,' said Longstint, 'I often look around and see things lying about. If I see them, I must have found them, but are they lost if someone else is looking for them?'

'If, however, nobody is looking for them, they can't be lost. Therefore, I must have found something that isn't lost.'

Yill was just about to tell Longstint that he

had answered his own question, when a shout went up from Bronglay.

'Lights in the trees,' he called out. 'Looks like the Yippets are here!'

All eyes turned to the forest, and sure enough, through the dark night appeared beams of orange lights, eerily flickering as the trees blocked them. The lights created huge moving shadows that seemed alive against the snowy ground.

Everything went strangely quiet as the Willigrews stood in a double line, facing the danger.

The silence did not last long though, as the Yippets broke cover and appeared at the edge of the forest. They gave out a loud, weird, scary sound, half song and half scream.

'LAAAAAAHAAAAAW.'

The trees shook. The ground shook, and so did the Willigrews.

The lights eventually found our little green army, frightened, but standing firm, awaiting instructions from Bronglay.

The Yippets approached, slowly at first, but seemed to gather speed as they advanced, their weapons pointing straight at the Willigrews.

'Mirrors ready,' shouted Bronglay and all the mirrors (and one courgette) were held aloft.

Bronglay then called to his little band, 'Steady the Willigrews.' Although he knew, in his heart, that nobody would run.

All too soon, the deadly beams were zapping the Willigrews, who all stood firm holding their mirrors in defiance.

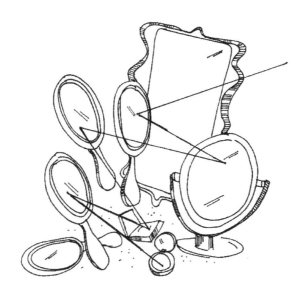

Disaster struck, the plan hadn't worked. Instead of reflecting the beams back onto the Yippets, the mirrors plus the courgette just disappeared.

The Yippets stopped firing for a moment; probably recharging their tortoises, then came forward for the last, deadly, attack.

Bronglay, fearing the worst, told his tribe to keep calm and be very brave.

'If we have to go we will go together, like true Willigrews,' he said, putting his arm around Yill.

Then they all held hands and marched toward the Yippets, knowing this would be the last adventure they would ever have.

Then to everyone's surprise, a little green flash broke ranks and ran toward the chickweed beds. It was Longstint.

Surely, Longstint wouldn't run away, thought the others. Not our brave Longstint.

But then, they saw him grab a big handful of chickweed and proceed to run toward the Yippets shouting, 'You won't beat the Willigrews.'

'Oh no,' cried Rewsin, 'Longstint's lost the plot.'

'I'm confused,' said Krowfin. Nobody was surprised at that.

Weaving and ducking to avoid any rays Longstint sprinted toward the Yippets. On reaching the first one, he shoved the chickweed into the mouth of the tortoise on its back.

The tortoise munched on the chickweed, saying, 'Yum, that's delicious. May I have some more please?' (Tortoises, in my experience, are always polite, I can say, honestly, that I have never met a rude tortoise, although I did meet a terrapin once that stuck its tongue out at me. Well, I did call it a turtle).

'Help yourself chum, it's over there,' said Longstint, pointing to the chickweed beds.

With that, the tortoise rolled off the Yippets back and headed for some more grub.

Before long the other tortoises followed, first one, then a few more, then all of them. Although some landed on their backs and had to be helped by the Willigrews, they were soon burrowing in the snow to get to the yummy chickweed.

All Willigrew eyes turned to the Yippets to see what they would do without their weapons.

Well, to everyone's surprise, they didn't do much at all. In fact, they all looked as confused as Krowfin on a bad day.

One Yippet did the 'LAAAAAAHAAAAAW' thing again, but this didn't seem as frightening now they had no weapons.

The first to approach the Yippets was Longstint. He stood directly in front of one and said, 'What are you going to do now, old mechanical spidery thing?'

'Not programmed for *what are you going to do now, old mechanical spidery thing*,' said the Yippet. 'This model not capable of rational thought. Model capable of rational thought available on manufacturer's website. Special offer this week only, interest free finance, subject to status, terms and conditions apply.'

'It's a computerised robot!' cried Longstint, turning to the other Willigrews with a look of surprise. 'They must be harmless without their tortoises.'

Krowfin then noticed that they had lids on their backs and decided to have a look inside. On opening the lid, he saw a switch, which was marked 'on and off'. Still feeling a bit nervous, he flicked the switch to the off position. The Yippet stopped moving completely and made no more sound.

Seeing this Bronglay instructed everyone to switch off all the Yippets.

So now, you have probably realised, the Willigrews had three problems.

a. How to get Georgie and Georgette back to their planet.

b. How to make sure they were safe from the other Yippets on their planet.

and

3. What to do with the empty Yippets in Willigrew.

Bronglay, as he usually does in such situations, called a meeting at the Meeting Hall.

He decided to hold the meeting on the day after tomorrow. If he called it tomorrow, it would be tomorrow, if you see what I mean, and if he called it on the day after tomorrow, it would be in two days' time.

In the end, he decided to call it on Wednesday, which was the day after Tuesday and two days before Friday.

A notice was pinned on the notice board (a pretty sensible place to put it), which read:

A MEETING TO DISCUSS OUR NEXT
MOVES REGARDING GEORGIE AND
GEORGETTE
WILL BE HELD ON
WEDNESDAY AT 9.30

WOULD EVERYONE BRING THEIR
THINKING CAPS
WE SUGGEST THE BLUE CAPS WITH THE
GREEN STRIPE IN ORDER TO KEEP UP
WITH THE LATEST FASHION
REFRESHMENTS WILL BE SERVED

AS THIS MEETING IS VERY IMPORTANT
ALL FURTHER NOTICES ARE POSTPONED
UNTIL FURTHER NOTICE

The weather was improving in Willigrew. The snow was melting quite quickly now, and the sun, although not warm, was shining brightly, which cheered everyone up.

Therefore, when everyone started to arrive at the Meeting Hall, there was a general feeling of hopefulness among the crowd that had gathered there.

They had all brought their thinking caps, all that is, except Zamborina. She explained that hers was in the wash, so instead she wore her pink one with the diamante dangly bits.

The refreshments were served, and, amid much munching and slurping and a small amount of guzzling, Bronglay, who was sitting between Georgie and Georgette, called the meeting to order.

'Good morning everyone,' he began, 'I think you all know why we are here. We have to decide what to do next. We have three things on the agenda and I think we should start by deciding what to do with the empty Yippets.'

'Give them a decent burial,' someone shouted from the back of the hall.

'Bronglay replied, 'Well, under normal circumstances, I would, but the Yippets are only machines and I don't think that would be appropriate.'

'Why don't we recycle them?' Came another shout from the back.

Cload, who was a bit hard of hearing didn't hear what was said, so he asked his wife who was sitting next to him. 'What did he say?'

'I think he wants to turn them into bicycles,' his wife, who was also a bit deaf, replied.

At which everyone laughed.

'I think,' suggested Yill, 'we should place them, tastefully around the village and put some nice bedding plants in them. They would really brighten things up in the spring and summer.'

A murmur of approval ran round the room,

ran round again then ran out of the door never to be seen again.

'Right,' said Bronglay, 'that's settled then. Now we need to decide how to get Georgie and Georgette back to their planet and how to save their people from the Yippets. Any ideas?'

'Why don't you use your magic, Bronglay?' asked Krowfin.

'That sounds like a good idea, but I don't think my magic would be strong enough to send them through outer space. Also, we couldn't be sure that they would be safe from the Yippets, even if they got there,' explained Bronglay.

Then Longstint spoke, 'Has anyone been to look at the spaceships that the Yippets arrived in? Perhaps we could send them back that way.'

'But, who would pilot the spaceship?' asked Krowfin.

'Not us,' replied Georgette, 'we haven't got a clue about flying things, but, if you need any bouncing up and down done, we are experts.'

'If bouncing is required,' answered Bronglay, 'we will certainly call on your superior bouncing skills straight away.'

Longstint (who else), was first to volunteer

to fly the spaceship, followed by Krowfin, Zamborina and Dora Dingbat.

Then, amidst all the excitement, spoke the voice of reason.

It was Yill, 'Just a little minute,' she warned. 'Do I sense a very dangerous adventure coming on?'

The hall fell silent, and listened.

'The Willigrews are brave and adventurous, but, this is something we have never done before. Are we all sure that not only flying to another planet but, more importantly, getting back, is something we are prepared to risk?' she continued.

'I'm up for it,' shouted Longstint, 'anyone else? Let's have a democratic vote.'

Bronglay agreed and asked for a show of hands.

'All those in favour of this dangerous mission, please raise your hands now,' he asked.

From the response, it looked like the majority wanted the mission to go ahead. However, Bronglay decided to give those against the chance to vote.

'All those against the dangerous mission, please raise your hands now.'

Just a few hands went up, so the mission was to go ahead.

'The Willigrews have spoken,' said Bronglay.

So plans were made for the journey into outer space.

The first thing to do was to cross the forest and find out about the space ships.

A small group of Willigrews came out of the trees to see the metallic spacecraft glinting in the sun.

They were not very big, ball-shaped with four windows.

Longstint was the first to climb into the cockpit of the nearest ship. Inside he found hundreds of controls and several flashing lights.

He approached the control board and sat in the seat provided and turned the on/off switch to the 'on' position.

Bronglay had joined Longstint and looked over his shoulder at the mass of lights and buttons.

'This is all very confusing,' said Longstint, 'how will we know which buttons to press?'

'I suppose we will have to take a chance and try some of them, otherwise how will we know?' replied Bronglay.

'Right, here goes nothing,' said Longstint, trying to look confident and not succeeding.

His hand hovered for a moment over a yellow button; he closed his eyes and pushed down with his finger.

For a moment, nothing happened, and then, to his surprise, the sound of music came from a speaker positioned in the roof.

The music was sort of jingly-jangly and really, quite pleasant so Longstint tried another button, this one being blue.

Again, more music, this time high-pitched jumpy-bouncy music.

'What is going on here?' asked Bronglay,

scratching his head (well it did itch a bit anyway).

'Hang on a bit,' said Longstint. 'I'll try some of the other buttons.'

So he did, with the same outcome, more music of all different types.

By now, there were only two buttons left to try. They were larger than the others, one red and one green.

'I will try the green one first,' said Longstint.

He pressed the button firmly, a bit more confident now.

No music this time but the whole space ship started to shake and there was a loud rumbling noise, which sounded a lot like the engines starting.

Then a mechanical sounding voice came from the speaker. 'Prepare for take-off. Co-ordinates set for the planet Byclipss, please fasten your seat belts and put your teacups down, ten seconds to take off.' Then the countdown started, '10, 9' etc.

'Oh yikes,' exclaimed Bronglay, 'we are going to take off, how do we stop it?'

Longstint, keeping calm, said, 'Only one button left, the red one, I'd better try it.'

'5, 4, 3,' the countdown continued relentlessly.

Longstint's finger approached the button and, just as the countdown reached one, he pressed the button down.

A few moments passed, and then the engine stalled and, eventually, stopped.

'Take-off aborted; you may remove your seat belts and pick up your teacups again. Thank you for listening,' announced the mechanical voice.

'Phew!' gasped Bronglay, wiping the perspiration from his forehead. 'That was a close one.'

'Too right mate,' agreed Longstint, 'but at least now we know how to start and stop this thing.'

'And you will have some nice musical entertainment on your journey,' enthused Bronglay.

Later on, when the Willigrews got back to their village, they held a meeting in order to choose the crew for the flight to Byclipss.

They decided that the crew would consist of Vectorn, Krowfin, Longstint and Dora Dingbat.

A list of items needed on the journey was

made and this is the very list:

Lots of chickweed products, including tea,
porridge and biscuits.
Plenty of jangleberry jam.
A few jars of air (in case there was no
atmosphere on Byclipss).
Some curly green wigs (to confuse the
Yippets).
Some curly red wigs (just in case the green
wigs didn't work).
A family size bag of chickweed leaves to feed to
the dangerous tortoises.
And finally, of course, Dora insisted on taking
a small twig in the shape of a mouse with two
legs missing.

This said Dora 'may not be of any use but might bring us luck.'

Early the next morning, which was shortly after the day before, the little band of trainee astronauts started to board the space ship.

A large crowd of Willigrews had gathered to see them off and Bronglay gave one of his speeches, which went something like this:

'Fellow Willigrews, this will be the greatest and most dangerous mission we have ever undertaken. It goes without saying how brave these Willigrews are, so I won't say it. Therefore it only remains for me to say Good Luck and please be very, very careful.'

Once Georgie and Georgette had thanked Bronglay, Yill and the rest, they bounced into the cockpit and made themselves comfortable by snuggling together on the floor and making little squeaking noises.

Longstint volunteered to fly the craft and sat awaiting instructions.

Vectorn pulled the door shut and turned the wheel, which sealed the cockpit shut.

'Are we all set?' asked Longstint, 'then off we go.'

He pressed the green button, and there followed a rumbling noise from the engines.

Then the mechanical words, 'Prepare for take-off. Co-ordinates set for the planet Byclipss, please fasten your seat belts and put your teacups down, ten seconds to take off.'

Then the countdown started as before, '10, 9, 8' etc.

'3, 2, 1, we have lift-off, lift-off starting, get ready for lift-off. If you are not ready for lift-off, it's too late; we are going to lift off anyway.'

'All right,' said Longstint, looking up at the speaker, 'we get your message, we are ready.'

Next came a loud whooshing sound (Dora was blowing her nose), after which a high-pitched whining, followed by a low-pitched whining then a medium pitched whining as the spaceship left the ground and ascended toward the sky.

'We're off,' cried Vectorn, 'Byclipss, here we come!'

All the Willigrews on board gathered around the back window, and watched the Earth shrink into the distance, until it became a small ball in the sky.

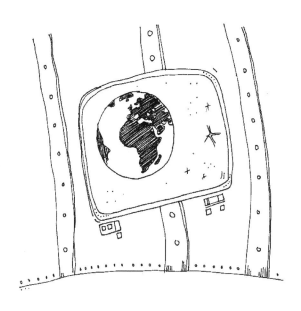

So beautiful in blue and green, this made the little group gasp in awe.

'That is the most amazing thing I have ever seen,' said Dora. 'I will never look at Earth in the same way again; I will probably stand on one leg with my fingers in my ears, and look at it that way.'

The others agreed and proceeded to do the Willigrew dance by hopping about on one leg and flicking their earlobes with their fingers, in excitement.

They had to stop however when the spaceship started to wobble about.

An announcement came from the speaker above. 'Craft wobbling, please stop moving about so much or it will go into a spin, which is not so good. Try some tai chi. Dancing bad, tai chi good.'

As the Willigrews didn't know what tai chi was, they decided to keep still, just to be on the safe side.

All was quiet, as our little band hurtled through space, until the silence was broken (Krowfin swept it up and put in the waste bin).

'Hazard up ahead,' called Longstint, in a worried voice. 'I don't know what it is but it looks a bit dangerous.'

'I don't like the sound of dangerous,' said Krowfin.

Just then, Dora asked, scratching her head, 'Does dangerous have a sound then, does it make a noise'

Nobody answered but Vectorn looked through the window, and what she saw filled her little green heart and part of her left foot, with terror!

'Is that gruesome, or what?' she said.

The others joined in the looking; up ahead in the distance they saw a gigantic, shapeless mass of a slimy, wet, glistening goo.

The speaker crackled, a new announcement, 'Goo Monster approaching, steer around it immediately, or you will all be gooed, which is most unpleasant and plays havoc with your nostrils!'

'I don't know about anyone else,' said Longstint, 'but I don't want any havoc up my nose.'

'The problem is, I don't know how to steer this thing, so we are heading straight for it. I think we should all cover our nostrils, just in case,' he said.

Just then, Vectorn had an idea. 'I have an idea,' she said (see, I told you she did), 'quickly, everyone get over to one side.'

They all rushed over to the left and stood against the wall.

Nothing happened for a few seconds and Vectorn could see the Goo Monster getting closer and closer.

Everyone stood waiting in terror, with their hands tightly grasping their nostrils, waiting for impact.

They were close enough now to hear the sound of the monster. A sort of disgusting slurping, sucking, which became louder as they grew closer to it.

Just then, the spaceship started to ease to the left.

Slowly at first and next, gathering speed it started to lurch toward the side of the hazard. Closer and closer, all held their breath.

They were still very much in danger, but Vectorn's plan had worked.

The ship avoided the main part of the Goo Monster and just clipped the side, leaving the horrible snot-like substance sticking to the windows.

'Hands off nostrils everyone, I think we are safe,' advised Vectorn.

As they did so, a revolting smell invaded

their little noses, a sort of cross between smelly cheese and a sausage that had been left out in the sun for two and three quarter days.

'What a whiff,' said Dora, holding her nose again, 'did anyone bring a peg?'

'Rather pungent,' said Vectorn, politely, 'now would everyone go back to their normal places?'

'Co-ordinates adjusted,' the speaker crackled, 'back on track for the planet Byclipss. That was a close shave, not that we spaceships shave at all. Just a figure of speech.'

Feeling much relieved, our little group decided to play some music, so Vectorn pressed one of the buttons, and waited.

The speaker did its usual crackly thing then, to everyone's delight started to sing a little song:

We're going back to Byclipss,
Where all good spaceships go,
And all the little Yippets,
Are standing in a row.

When we get back to Byclipss,
We will get some oil,
Then we'll have a little rest,
From all these weeks of toil.

Yum de dum de doo dah,
Do de dum de dah,
Yum te tum de do dee,
Rum te tum te tah.

Everyone clapped their hands in time with the song, except for Georgie and Georgette, who bounced up and down making little squeaking sounds, which is, after all, what they do.

Then Longstint said, 'Very nice tune, but the lyrics could do with some work.'

Not much happened for a while, in fact they were all getting a bit bored, just looking out at space.

At one point Dora did think she saw a giant giraffe, wearing a party dress and Doc Martins go by but it just turned out to be a bit of the goo stuck to the window, so everyone went back to being bored.

Even Georgie and Georgette were bored, Georgette saying 'I am so bored I don't even feel like bouncing, do you know I haven't got a single bounce in me let me tell you, which is very unusual for a Mardronian.'

'I know,' shouted Dora, 'let's play a game of something.'

'How do you play that, I've never played 'something' before, could you teach me the rules?' asked Vectorn excitedly.

However, before Dora could explain, the mechanical voice crackled into life saying, 'Attention, danger, warning, take care and big alarms and that sort of stuff. Very bad thing ahead, do not know what it is but we are heading straight for it! Help, I want my mum.'

Longstint looked out of the window and, what he saw made him very fearful.

Directly ahead, he saw a huge black and yellow ball. It seemed to be pulsing and throbbing, with streaks of light flashing outwards.

It was big, very big. So big, it would make something gigantic look nowhere near as big as this was.

'Oh-oh!' Longstint warned, 'we have a bit of a problem here, everyone. I don't think we will be able to steer around this big boy, we are heading straight for it.'

'What can we do?' asked Dora, waving her twig in the shape of a mouse with two legs missing, in the air, in the hope that it would bring them luck. It didn't.

Vectorn instructed everyone to lie down on

the floor and cover their heads.

All, that is except Longstint did so. Longstint stayed at his post, bravely still trying to find a way to steer the ship.

It was no use, the ship seemed to gather pace as it approached the danger and, finally, it slammed into the big mass of whatever it was, and plunged our little band deep into it.

Inside the space ship, everything went dark and quiet.

'Where are we?' asked Georgette, sounding frightened.

Her answer came from the mechanical voice, which Krowfin had decided to call Sidney, after his uncle Wilfred.

'We have carried out an analysis and have decided that we have entered a Gas Giant, or, as it is known in some quarters a Jovian planet. Hooray!'

'The good news is we should pass safely through and out the other side,' it continued.

'Boo! The bad news is it will take us 17.356921 recurring years.'

Longstint wondered how long a recurring year was.

Nobody answered his query. They all sat quietly, waiting for someone else to speak.

They all felt pretty helpless and, to be honest were starting to think that they were doomed.

Just then, as their eyes became accustomed to the gloom, they noticed Georgie bouncing up and down by the control panel. He then started to hover in front of a panel in the space ship's wall.

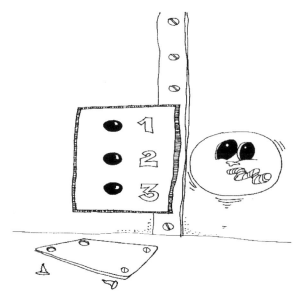

'I wonder what's in here?' he asked, 'let's try opening it, it may be important.'

'I'll take a look,' said Longstint, and proceeded to loosen the four screws that held the panel in place. It fell to the floor with a clang, which made Vectorn jump a bit.

What they saw inside was a bit strange. Three buttons, numbered one, two and three.

Before they could discuss what the numbers meant, Sidney (the mechanical voice) crackled again, before saying, 'Three buttons, button one is warp factor fairly fast, button two is warp factor faster than button one but not as fast as button three and button three is warp factor faster than buttons one and two so hold on to your hats. Explaining..., g-force will be high, giving you very squashy faces.'

Finally, it said, 'If you don't mind squashiness of the face, go for it, press button three. Thank you for listening,'

Vectorn spoke, 'I don't think we have a choice, we must risk it. Otherwise, we are doomed, condemned, damned and, in short, we have had our chips!'

'Ooh! I fancy a chip right now,' said Longstint, 'I am feeling a bit peckish.'

'I don't remember eating any chips,' Krowfin said, feeling a bit deprived of sustenance.

After a democratic vote, in which everybody agreed with Vectorn, Longstint stood in front of the buttons and, his hand shaking a little, pressed button number three.

'Brace yourselves, prepare for squashy faces,' warned Sidney.

'Everybody braced?' shouted Vectorn, over the noise of the engines, 'let's go for it.'

Then came all sorts of whooshing, rumbling and several varieties of whining, and they were off, hurtling through the Gas Giant towards freedom.

As the g-forces kicked in all the Willigrews faces became distorted and very squashy, their little round faces looking like deflated green footballs.

The Mardronians, however, were unaffected and thought it all very amusing, bouncing up and down and squeaking excitedly.

Suddenly, the darkness receded and Sidney crackled again, 'We have left the Gas Giant, arriving at Byclipss in precisely ten minutes thirty three seconds, please prepare for landing, which might be a bit bumpy.'

'What a relief,' sighed Dora, 'have we got our faces back yet?'

'I've just got to move my nose back to the middle, it's stuck behind my ear,' said Krowfin. 'Ooh, ouch! That's it, all back to normal now.'

By now, Georgie and Georgette were becoming very excited as they approached their home planet.

'Hold on tight,' said Sidney, 'we are about to land, get ready for the Byclipss bumps.'

The space ship landed with a huge thump, followed by a rolling motion that sent the Willigrews flying around, bumping into the walls and each other before, finally, coming to a stop, fortunately the right way up.

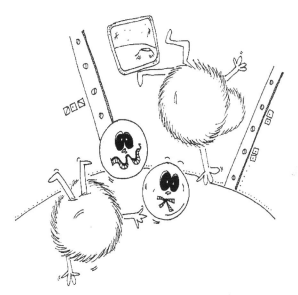

'Everyone all right?' asked Vectorn, brushing down her fur.

Krowfin was the first to venture outside, followed by Dora and the rest.

What they saw was amazing, miles and miles of very tall green sparkling grassy fields. The sun was shining, the sky was blue and the birds were singing.

'This could be paradise,' said Vectorn, with a dreamy look in her eyes.

The Mardronians bounced about, squeaking and whooping with delight, they were so happy to be back home.

Everything seemed calm and peaceful until, suddenly, without warning the peace was broken by something jumping out of the long grass.

Big and metallic, it shouted 'yippet!' then disappeared back where it came from.

Then another jumped up with another 'yippet!'

Before long, there were Yippets everywhere, hundreds of them, appearing and disappearing, all shouting 'yippet!'

'Yippet, yippet, yippet, yippet, yippet,' they went.

The noise was deafening.

'Run for your lives,' screeched Georgette, 'the Yippets are coming.'

Not needing a second invitation, the Willigrews and the Mardronians all climbed quickly back into the space ship and closed the hatch.

'Was that close, or what?' said Longstint, panting. 'What are we going to do now?'

Sidney crackled into life again, 'Do not wish to be a pessimist, but there is no defence against the Yippets, so you are all, more than likely, going to die.'

'Thanks for that,' replied Krowfin. 'Very cheerful, I'm sure. If you think we are done for, you don't know the Willigrews. We will think of something, won't we Vectorn?'

They all turned and looked, expectantly, at Vectorn, who was, after all, their leader on this expedition.

Vectorn suggested that they wait until dark. She thought that there was a better chance of sneaking away from the Yippets then.

They all settled down; while Krowfin prepared some jangleberry jam sandwiches and chickweed tea.

Amidst the munching and slurping Longstint said that he had noticed the Yippets didn't have the dangerous tortoises on their backs, and wondered if they would be as big a threat as they had been in Willigrew.

Georgie informed him that the Yippets in Willigrew were just robot machines but the ones on Byclipss were the deluxe models, programmed for rational thought.

He also told Longstint that they still had the dangerous tortoises but only used them in certain circumstances. Georgie explained further however, that in the old days, before they bred the tortoises, the Yippets were quite harmless and friendly.

'So,' remarked Vectorn, 'if we can disarm or perhaps make friends with the tortoises we may solve the Mardronians problems.'

'Indeed,' replied Georgette, 'that would be wonderful.'

As night fell, the little troupe prepared to leave the space ship.

They were all getting ready to open the hatch, when the craft started to move.

Slowly, at first then more quickly, and before long they were moving across the ground at some speed.

'Something is lifting us away,' shouted Georgette, looking out of the window, 'but there is nobody out there, we are just floating.'

They checked all the windows but saw nothing. They were baffled, but thought, hopefully that this would, at least, get them away from the Yippets.

This unexpected journey lasted for quite a while until, eventually, the craft came to a stop.

Everyone looked up at the hatch, not knowing what to expect, when the sound of movement was heard.

The hatch opened and a voice said, 'Welcome to Byclipss, you are safe now, until the Yippets find us. You can come out now.'

All the Willigrews and the Mardronians clambered outside but were amazed that there was nobody there.

They were wondering who had opened the hatch and who had spoken, when a voice said, 'Sorry to confuse you but we are invisible, thanks to the dangerous tortoises.'

Georgie and Georgette recognised the voice immediately and became very excited.

'Are my mum and dad with you?' asked Georgette.

'No, but we will take you to them now, they have missed you very much and can't wait to see you again. They will be delighted that you are both safe,' the voice replied.

The 'voice' said his name was Grendacx

and that he would find out the Willigrews names when they were safe.

'No time for introductions now,' said Grendacx, 'you must follow me as closely as you can. You will be able to see where I am by the movement in the long grass.'

The grass separated, as if by magic, as the Willigrews very quietly walked behind Grendacx.

After about fifteen minutes, they came to a large straw hut, covered in what seemed to be, a glass dome.

As they approached, Grendacx told them all to wait, and then he said, in a whisper, 'groidenbider'.

No sooner had he spoken than an opening appeared in the glass dome.

They all went through and it closed behind them.

As soon as they entered the hut, Georgie and Georgette started bouncing up and down and squeaking loudly, 'Mum, Dad, we have missed you so much; it's wonderful to be back.'

Because, although their parents were invisible, they could recognise their voices.

'Oh! My little darlings,' said their mum, 'we have been so worried, we thought we would never see you again.'

This was followed by much visible bouncing and even more invisible bouncing.

When the bouncing, boinging, squeaking and general silliness quietened down, Vectorn said she would introduce the Willigrews to their new friends.

She went around, each in turn, and told the Mardronians their names.

Grendacx replied by pointing at spaces and introducing the members of his tribe.

'This space is Mardih and this space is Groonbagga.' These were followed by Lobjount, Wakefine, Lowgraine and, finally, Baydrecx.

She explained that these were the

Mardronians who carried the space ship back to the dome, and said the rest of the tribe were hidden in tunnels under the long grass.

'We are very grateful, I'm sure,' said Dora.

The rest agreed and gave them a round of applause, (although, as they were standing in a square, perhaps that should be, a square of applause).

Anyway, they all clapped in a 'thank you very much' sort of way.

After this, everyone sat down and had some food, (the Mardronians loved the jangleberry dodgy jammers by the way) and talked about how the Willigrews could help the Mardronians solve the problem of the evil Yippets.

Many dangers lay ahead for the Willigrews, but, as always they were up for the challenge.

Grendacx explained to the Willigrews that for many years, they had lived in peace with the Yippets. 'We never bothered them and they never bothered us,' he said.

He went on to say, 'One morning, as some of my tribe and I were gathering seeds from the tall grass fields, we were confronted by the Yippets. This was fairly normal, and we waved hello. However, to our surprise, they had tortoises on their backs.'

'We were amused at first, thinking it was just a game of some sort. We stopped laughing, however, when the tortoises fired laser beams at us. Then one by one, we started to disappear.'

Grendacx continued, 'I managed to avoid the rays for a time by dodging in and out of the grass, but, eventually, they hit me, and we were all invisible. We managed to run away back to our home and, thankfully, the Yippets didn't follow us, just made their scary 'Ooolaah' sound as we fled.'

Grendacx explained further that the only Mardronians that were visible were Georgie and Georgette. 'So we decided to send them away in the space eggs, in the hope that they would land somewhere that was safe from the Yippets,' he continued.

'You see, we didn't know if the invisibility was permanent. Until you disappear you don't realise how difficult, almost impossible it is to live without seeing each other. We have to do everything by sound and touch.'

Vectorn then asked, 'Have you any idea what made the Yippets change so suddenly?'

Wakefine answered, 'We did think one thing was a bit strange. You see, at night they used to sleep where they stopped, out in the fields. One night, however, they all gathered in one place. The next morning we awoke to find that a huge metal structure had been erected in the field opposite our home.'

'We sneaked over to take a look, and were puzzled to see all the Yippets crouching down, facing the structure. A large door opened, and out came the tortoises and climbed on the Yippets backs. Then they all headed off in the same direction.'

Longstint, who had been sitting quietly listening to all this, joined in by saying, 'I have an idea of what is going on here. I think that whatever has changed the Yippets is controlling them from the new structure. I wouldn't mind taking a sneaky peek inside.'

What followed could only be called a chorus of disapproval.

'That would be far too dangerous,' warned Vectorn, and the rest agreed.

'But it's the only way we will be able to find out what's going on. We can't just sit and wait for something to happen. I will go now while it's dark. I promise I won't take any unnecessary risks,' Longstint continued.

'You can't go on your own,' said Dora Dingbat. 'I will come with you to hold your hand, just in case you get a bit frightened.'

'All right,' said Vectorn, reluctantly, 'but take some jangleberry dodgy jammer biscuits with, we don't want you starving.'

'You had better take one of us with you,' advised Grendacx, 'to show you the way. Who wants to go? It may be dangerous.'

They must have all volunteered because Grendacx said, 'You can't all go. I think Groonbagga should go; he is our best tracker.'

The decision made the brave little trio set off into the night, through the long grass toward the structure. They trundled along, following Groonbagga's movements, until they reached the edge of a clearing.

There, before them, stood a gigantic five-sided building which looked like it was constructed of some sort of thick paper, and was decorated with floral wallpaper.

Longstint remarked, 'I like this wallpaper design, it's rather chic, I would love it on my walls at home.'

Dora reminded him why they were there and told him to concentrate on the job at hand.

'OK,' Longstint replied, 'I'm focussed now. We need to find the entrance, follow me.'

They edged stealthily around the building until they came upon a small opening between the structure and the ground.

Longstint squeezed under it, and the others followed. On the inside, it was quite dark with only a probing light beam coming from the top of a tower in the centre.

The light moved around the edge of the building and approached our little heroes.

'Duck,' Groonbagga called out, urgently.

'Eh, what would a duck be doing in here?' said Dora, feeling a bit confused.

However, she realised just in time what he meant and joined Longstint on the ground as the beam passed above their heads.

They then saw that all the Yippets were inside the building, not moving, but barring the way to the tower, possibly asleep.

'We will have to make our way over to the tower,' explained Longstint, 'I need to take a look inside. We will have to go between the Yippets' legs, so be very careful.'

'OK?' whispered Dora, 'ready, steady, go.'

The trio dashed across the ground, dodging and weaving as quietly as they could between the metal legs, before the beam traced them.

However, suddenly there was a bump and Groonbagga gave out a loud groan. The others stopped and asked if he was all right, but he didn't answer.

Longstint tried to locate the little invisible Mardronian by scrabbling around on the ground.

Eventually he found Groonbagga. 'Are you OK old chap?' Longstint asked.

Getting no reply he said, 'I think he's unconscious Dora, we will have to leave him here and collect him on our way out.'

Before they left the unfortunate Mardronian, Dora had the clever idea of sticking her small twig in the shape of a mouse with two legs missing, in the ground next to Groonbagga, so they would know where he was when they came back. 'I knew it would come in handy,' she thought to herself, rather smugly.

As Longstint passed the Yippets, he noted with interest that they had cables running from them connected to the tower.

When they got to the tower, the only entrance, they could see was about half a metre above the ground, far too high for a Willigrew to reach.

They were stumped. 'I'm stumped,' said Dora.

'Me too,' said Longstint. (See, I told you they were).

They looked about for something to use, but all they could see was a small plank of wood, which was flat and a bit bendy.

They both stared at the object for a few minutes, then, Longstint had an idea, 'What if we lean it up against the wall and use it as a trampoline? We may be able to spring up to the entrance and dive in.'

Dora thought this was a bit dangerous but said she was up for it.

Once they had positioned the plank at, what they considered would be the correct angle; Longstint took a run-up and dashed toward it.

He jumped with both feet and landed in the middle. 'Boing' it went and he flew upwards at great speed and disappeared into the opening. A loud, squeaky bump followed and an 'ouch!'

Dora followed with another squeaky bump, but missed the opening and squashed her nose against the wall.

However, her second attempt was successful, and the Willigrews were inside the tower.

Dora's nose was bleeding but this didn't stop her following Longstint to the small building at the centre of the tower.

This time there was a door, that wasn't locked. Longstint opened it, with a creak, (he always carried a creak with him, in case he needed to open a door).

Dora's eyes widened at what she saw. On one side of the room was a large computer-like thingy. 'Look Longstint,' she said, 'it's a computer-like thingy, what can that be used for?'

Longstint edged closer to take a look, but was stopped in his tracks when, above him, sitting on top of the computer-like thingy, was what could only be described as a purple blob with two eyes, a button nose and a wide, grinning mouth.

It spoke 'Who dares enter the inner sanctum of The Mighty Nawg, ruler of all known worlds, the whole universe and parts of Watford?'

'Keep your hands off my computer-like

thingy, or you will be in big trouble and no mistake.'

The Willigrews knew they had a problem, so, Dora, as a last resort offered Nawg a jangleberry dodgy jammer.

'I don't eat,' roared Nawg, 'I am a fungus.'

'Well, I never,' said Longstint, 'I've never met a fungus before, well, not to speak to anyway.'

'I will give you one warning and one warning only, leave at once or I will fungulate you with my fungulator, and you won't like that very much, I can tell you,' Nawg roared again.

'I don't like the sound of that,' said Dora, nervously. 'Show us what you mean.'

The angry Nawg, from a tube on the top of his head, fired a warning shot above Dora's head. A long spurt of green slimy stuff hit the wall behind them and immediately produced a large gaping hole.

'Keep him busy somehow,' said Longstint, 'I want to take a look at this computer-like thingy.'

'Do you want to play games?' enquired Dora, trying desperately trying to sound defiant.

Nawg fired another salvo, but missed as Dora dashed about trying to avoid the deadly fungus.

'Yah! Never touched me,' she shouted.

Nawg tried again, this time nearly hitting his target. Dora, in trying to keep moving tripped and fell. Nawg took careful aim, and, with a triumphant smirk on his face fired his fungulator.

In the nick of time Dora rolled sideways to safety. She was becoming tired and felt that she couldn't keep this up for much longer when, to her relief, Nawg stopped fungulating and went quiet.

'Whoopee,' cried Longstint, 'I think I've got it sorted. I have disconnected the programmerator from the flange-grommet.'

Nawg spoke, very slowly, slurring his words, 'what have you done, you meddlesome green things, I'm feeling a bit dodgy now. Who will control the universe now, oh well, such is life.'

The Willigrews looked intently at Nawg and, to be honest, felt a bit sorry for him. He was starting to melt, slowly at first but then he was starting to disintegrate, his fungussy body running down the sides of the computer-like thingy.

Then, when he had almost melted completely, there was a small pop and what was left exploded. Finally, as the last bits plopped over the computer-like thingy, he was gone, never more to carry out his evil fungal doings.

Both the Willigrews were feeling very sad. They didn't like hurting creatures, let alone killing them.

They walked away, shoulders drooping to help Groonbagga, when, suddenly, out of what seemed like nowhere, they heard a tiny high-pitched voice say pleadingly, 'Please don't leave me behind, not now that I have escaped the smelly fungus.'

Dora and Longstint were amazed to see, sitting on the keyboard of the computer-like thingy, a Mardronian.

'Hello, where did you come from little round creature?' enquired Dora in a gentle voice.

The Mardronian explained, a bit shakily, that his name was Griddlebucx; he had been captured by the fungus while walking in the fields one day and could not escape.

'You see, a fungus can't think or talk without a living creature inside it,' Griddlebucx explained. 'It was using my voice and brain to carry out its evil deeds. Thank you so much for rescuing me.'

The Willigrews introduced themselves and went out to see how Groonbagga was. When they reached him he had regained consciousness, was glad to see his new friends, and was especially happy to see Griddlebucx again, whom it turned out had been missing for a very long time.

But, what of the Yippets? They were still not moving. Longstint had a look inside one and it appeared to be dead. He suggested that perhaps they only worked when the computer-like thingy was controlling them.

However, as he walked past them he accidentally kicked one of the cables and disconnected it.

Immediately, the Yippet came to life. The Willigrews stood back in fear but need not have worried, as it said, 'We owe you a great debt of gratitude, you lovely little green fluffers. You have set us free from The Mighty Nawg, and now we can be friends with the lovely Mardronians again.'

Once disconnected the Yippets followed the Willigrews back.

The motley band made their way back to

the dome, following Groonbagga through the long grass when, to Longstint's surprise and delight the invisible Mardronian started to reappear.

It wasn't long before he was back in full view. Of course, he was overjoyed and bounced up and down and squeaked, in the usual Mardronian way.

When they got back, everyone was waiting, outside the dome, to welcome the heroes back.

The Mardronians were visible again and bouncing up and down, excitedly. The Willigrews, of course were doing their customary dance, hopping about on one leg and flicking their earlobes with their index fingers.

The Yippets joined in by waving their two front legs in the air and making their 'ooolah' sound again, but this time in a happy melodic way.

Now, I hear you ask, what became of the dangerous tortoises? Well, during the dancing and bouncing, a large tortoise appeared through the long grass. This worried both the Willigrews and the Mardronians, not to mention the Yippets.

Sorry, I said I wouldn't mention them.

The first tortoise approached the crowd of revellers, and said 'We are sorry for all the nasty things that Nawg made us do. We are now harmless unless required to be otherwise. We have vowed to protect Byclipss and all its inhabitants from danger, whatever it might be, from this day forward.'

Everybody cheered as all the other tortoises appeared through the long grass.

Dora decided then, to hand out the green and red wigs and everyone tried them on, even the Yippets.

Well it seemed a shame, after bringing them all this way, not to use them.

The returning group joined in and a happy time was had by all.

With all the problems sorted out, the next problem was how to get the Willigrews back home.

Vectorn suggested that they use the same space ship that they came in, but Grendacx said he had a much better craft that they could use.

When the Willigrews saw it, they were very impressed. This was no little cramped round thing, but a sleek, silver, state-of-the-art machine that, the Mardronians explained, would get them back safely in double-quick time.

There were tears from all the tribes when, finally, the Willigrews climbed on board to make their journey home.

Longstint pressed the 'lift-off' button and, with everyone waving, the space ship shot skyward, leaving Byclipss behind and heading home to Willigrew.

At first, the journey was uneventful, although the crew were much more comfortable in this ship, it being much more spacious and having all mod cons, like armchairs, very nice toilets and excellent cooking facilities.

Everyone was relaxing, some nodding off, when the old familiar crackling speaker sprung into life. 'Danger up ahead,' it barked, 'giant space amoeba up ahead, avoid, avoid at all costs.'

Explaining..., 'please wait.' Silence, then another crackle and the warning followed.

'We are about to encounter a giant space amoeba or, if you prefer, a cosmoamoeba. Hooray! The good news is that it is contracted which means it is only about half a kilometre wide. Boo! The bad news is you still have to get around it.'

'By the way, if it was extended it could be more than ten kilometres wide, which is interesting, so think yourselves lucky, but take immediate action to avoid it.'

'Oh! No, what shall we do?' asked Longstint, as they hurtled toward the danger.

'Oh! Sorry.' said Sidney, 'how silly of me, I forgot to mention, if you like you can turn on 'auto-pilot' and the ship will do it all for you.'

Despite the danger, Krowfin was so pleased because the mechanical voice sounded like his old mate Sidney.

'Hi Sidney old mate, how's it going with you?' asked Krowfin.

Sidney replied, 'Not too bad, Krowfin, old pal, thanks for asking.'

Dora complained that Krowfin was passing the time of day with Sidney, when they could be heading for disaster.

'Sorry, just being friendly,' was Krowfin's reply.

Longstint scanned the control panel, carefully, and, eventually found a button marked 'AUTO PILOT, only press if you want 'auto pilot', if you do not want 'auto pilot', do not press. If you want something other than

'Auto Pilot', you will have to press a different button.'

Not surprisingly, Longstint pressed the button, and the space ship immediately veered sharply to the left, which sent all the Willigrews rolling to one side. They ended up in an untidy heap on the floor.

They soon got back up, however, and gathered around a window, just in time to see the giant space amoeba as they passed by.

'Wow,' said Vectorn, 'it looks like a giant jellyfish, with a long tail. It is quite beautiful really. I suppose though, that many beautiful things are dangerous.'

The others agreed, then settled back to enjoy the rest of the flight.

Sidney only sounded one more alarm on the way back to Willigrew. 'Large mass of objects heading our way; could be meteorites. Big danger if big objects. Analysing as we speak, please wait.' warned Sidney.

Another few moments of silence, then 'Very strange phenomenon, appears to consist of flour, water and suet, objects not in my memory bank!'

The Willigrews gathered round the window again and saw several quite large round objects approaching.

'Wait a minute,' said Krowfin, smiling, 'I think they might be dumplings, what are dumplings doing in outer space?'

As he spoke, one of the dumplings hit the side of the ship with a loud plop, followed by a slurping sound as it slipped down the side.

'They are definitely dumplings,' Dora confirmed, 'and I've got a theory.'

The others seemed to show some interest, so she continued, 'I think these are a group of Cosmo dumplings that are roaming the universe trying to find a beef stew or maybe a chicken casserole to join up with. I wouldn't mind betting that somewhere in space there is a giant casserole wandering around looking for dumplings.'

Nobody seemed convinced by Dora's theory, but didn't have time to discuss the subject as Sidney interrupted.

'Prepare for landing in precisely seven minutes and nine seconds. Please take all your belongings with you on leaving the ship. I hope you have enjoyed your trip on Sidney's airline and trust you will travel with us again in the near future. Thank you for listening and goodbye.'

The Willigrews became very excited as Willigrew came into view. They all cheered, and were so glad to be home again.

The landing was uneventful and, finally, our little band of green friends stepped out of the space ship.

A large crowd, headed by Yill and Bronglay, who had arranged a big party with funny hats and chickweed champagne, greeted them.

At the party, Bronglay made one of his customary speeches, which went quite a bit like this:

'My dear Willigrews, I think I speak for everyone when I say how grateful we are to the brave Willigrews who went to Byclipss to save the Mardronians. They are all heroes, and we welcome them home.'

'Just one more thing, I think the first dance should be a bouncy one, in honour of our new friends the Mardronians.'

'Now, let us all enjoy the party.'

So, we will leave the Willigrews dancing and singing, following another exciting, successful and very silly adventure.

The End

THE WILLIGREWS AND THE ALIEN ENCOUNTER

You may not know this, but in Willigrew, during springtime, there is a special week, every year, when a dense, sparkling mist surrounds the village.

The Willigrews call this time Mistival and arrange all sorts of activities, as part of the celebration.

The activities are, more or less, the same every year. There are, among others, pin the donkey on the tail (not a real donkey of course), who can jump the highest while eating three sausages, who can melt most ice cubes using just their earlobes and, of course, the old favourite, who can make the most words from the word floccinaucinihilipilification?

At this year's Mistival, the Willigrews had invited some of their friends, the Dranglebinders, to join them in the fun and games

Everybody seemed to be enjoying themselves, amidst much laughter and general silliness, when Partive, who had been standing outside the mist, came running up to Bronglay shouting, 'Something is landing in the chickweed beds; it's very big and shiny, like a big shiny gravy boat type of thing!'

Bronglay, Partive and Yill ran over to the chickweed beds and saw exactly what Partive had described. It did not land; however, and was just hovering, several metres off the ground.

By now, several other Willigrews and some Dranglebinders had gathered to take a look.

'What do you think it is?' asked Longstint, 'could it be aliens from a distant planet?'

Before anyone could answer, a little female Dranglebinder ran out and stood beneath the shiny craft. Bronglay acted quickly and sprinted over to the rescue.

Sadly, he was too late; before he could reach her, a beam of blue light zapped the child. In less than a split second, she was gone and the craft shot up to the sky at lightning speed, disappearing behind the clouds.

Everyone stood, silently staring at the spot where Morwixx had been, when her father Flindax came pushing through the crowd.

He walked over to where his daughter had been and said tearfully, 'Morwixx was my only child; she can't be gone, what am I going to do?'

He fell to his knees and placed his hand on the ground, and, to his surprise, touched a small box of some sort. He picked it up and inspected it. After reading the label, which said 'Chicken Tikka Masala', in realisation he looked, despairingly up to the sky and cried. 'They have turned my beloved daughter into a ready meal!'

A crowd gathered around Flindax, and tried their best to console him. However, he was totally distraught and cradling the box in his arms; he headed off toward his village.

Longstint walked beside him for a while and heard him speaking, tearfully, to his unfortunate, transformed 'daughter'.

'I will never forget you, my love, and I promise that, no matter how hungry I become; I will never cook you on a high heat for three minutes in the microwave.'

Nobody felt like carrying on with the Mistival celebrations after that, so all the Dranglebinders went home. When they had gone, Bronglay gathered a group of friends together at his house in order to discuss the plight of poor Morwixx.

They all sat around the kitchen table. Bronglay made them all a cup of chickweed tea, and they just looked at each other, shocked and very sad.

Yill was first to speak, saying, 'Do you really think it is possible to turn a living creature into a ready meal?'

Krowfin replied, 'Well they are, as far as we know, aliens and I suppose it's possible. Who knows how advanced they are on whatever planet they come from? Perhaps they can do it the other way around and turn ready meals into living creatures.'

Bronglay, looking rather serious, held his hands up, palms forward, trying to calm everyone, and said, 'All our wondering and asking questions won't help. We cannot possibly know what these aliens are capable of, so we must think of a way to find them and put things right for the Dranglebinders.'

Just then, there was a gentle tapping sound at the front door. Dora opened it and in flew Duffy Scrunnock, the little bird who now lived, for part of the year, in Willigrew.

'Hello everyone,' chirped Duffy, 'I couldn't help hearing with my highly sensitive, superior birdie ears that you need someone to look for the aliens. Well, look no further than Duffy, my friends. Don't forget, I can fly a long way and would be pleased to carry out a search on your behalf.'

'Are you sure,' asked Longstint, 'it could be very dangerous; they might turn you into an oven-ready Scrunnock, and we would not like that?'

'I'll risk it for my mates,' said Duffy, twitching.

Yill smiled, 'We are so lucky to have a Scrunnock like you, as a friend.'

It is impossible to tell when a bird blushes, due to the feathers, but I think Duffy did, just then. Following that, with much waving and good lucking from the Willigrews, he flapped a cheery good-bye and flew up above the forest before disappearing into the distance.

He flapped and glided, glided and flapped high above the earth, soaring up then swooping down to look at what was on the ground between the trees.

After a while, our little feathered friend started to feel a bit peckish so decided to land upon the ground to find something to eat. He searched around on the grass, twitching and hopping, until he found what he was looking for.

Some kind creature had put some birdseed out, and he tucked in, gratefully pecking up the tasty treat, along with a few small insects that happened to be passing by.

'Right,' thought Duffy, 'better get back to the job in hand,' then flew, effortlessly skyward to continue his search, singing a little song as he went.

Fly, fly, fly,
All I do is fly,
I don't know why,
I'm always passing by.

Sometimes I stop,
Then I twitch and hop,
Fly, hop, twitch,
It doesn't matter which.

This little ditty seemed to cheer Duffy up, and he flew a bit more quickly until he spotted something with his extremely sharp eyes. There was something on the ground in a clearing among some trees.

Unable to make it out, he flew lower and landed on a branch. Peering through the leaves, he was now able to see the object more clearly.

'OK,' he said to himself, 'I am looking for a sizeable metallic craft, and that is definitely a sizeable metallic craft. The craft I am looking for should be in the shape of a gravy boat, and that is certainly gravy boat shaped. Both boxes ticked; I think I have found it.'

As he watched, he noticed a sliding door was open, so he flew down and looked inside.

What he saw made him feel a bit queasy, the floor, the walls and the ceiling were all covered in a yellowish-green slime, which moved about, slurping and dripping sickeningly.

'Err, gross!' gasped Duffy, not noticing that something was moving behind him until he saw its shadow.

In a bit of a panic he flew into the bushes very quickly, then turned and looked back. What he saw was, he thought, double gross.

It wasn't a slug and it wasn't a lizard, but both in one body. Duffy couldn't decide whether to think of it as luggard or a slizard.

The front part of its body was upright with a lizardy face and scaly claws; its rear was like a large slug. It moved quite slowly, leaving a trail of yellow slime, which steamed, moved and slithered about on the grass.

Just then, another one joined it and sliding up beside it, started to talk. Duffy couldn't understand the language, which sounded like, 'mrarma, mrorga, malplang.'

Even their speech was slimy, somewhat gurgling and, much more disgusting, was the yellow slime dripping from their lips as they spoke.

'Slimy, or what?' thought Duffy,' I had better go back and report my findings to the Willigrews.'

However, just as he was about to leave, he noticed that more of the slimy creatures had appeared and were busy loading crates of something into the gravy-boat thing. The crates were quite large and tied with metal tape.

Duffy took off and was soon soaring, quickly into the sky, feeling quite excited and intrigued about what he had seen. On the way back he had to hide in a tree for a while until a Harrowspawk, which is the Scrunnocks' number one enemy, had gone.

After that, it didn't take him long to fly home to Willigrew.

Yill had seen him coming and opened the door. He flew straight onto the kitchen table and started to peck at a jangleberry muffin, which Yill had prepared for his return, thinking he was sure to be hungry after his long flight.

'Yum, yum, jelly bum,' said Duffy, 'Thanks Yill that was double delish, in fact, it was jangletastic.'

Yill and Duffy were joined by Bronglay, who, on entering said, 'Hello Duffers, old feathery chap, did you find the aliens?'

'I certainly did,' replied Duffy, 'and a right weird bunch they are too, and no mistake.'

He then went on to give Bronglay and Yill a full, detailed report of what he had seen in the clearing.

He also suggested that some of the Willigrews should go to the aliens' hideout in order to make further enquiries.

Bronglay scratched his head, 'Well, if we are to find out what happened to poor Morwixx, I am afraid you are right Duffy. I'll call a meeting and ask for volunteers.'

They held the meeting, appropriately enough, in the Meeting Hall. Most of the village attended, which was not surprising considering how upset, they all were by what had happened and were eager to help in any way they could.

'I am sorry to pull you all away from the sparkling mist,' Bronglay began, 'but, as you know, Duffy has been out searching for the aliens, if that is what they are, and has found them. With your agreement, I would like to gather a team of about a half a dozen of you to go and meet them and see what we can do to find out what they actually did to little Morwixx.'

'According to Duffy's report, these creatures are very slimy and could be dangerous so, I will not blame anyone for not wanting to go. Now, all those who wish to join the mission, please raise your hands.'

It came as no surprise to Bronglay that every hand was raised, except that is for Repscar's, who was a self-confessed wimp and would probably hide under a blanket until the party came back, just to be on the safe side.

After much discussion, drawing of lots, drawing of littles and walking around in square circles, the final list was Bronglay, Krowfin, Longstint, Dora, Rewsin and Duffy.

Very early, the next morning as the sun was starting to show through the sparkling mist, the little band assembled on the edge of the village.

A small crowd had gathered to see them off and, with much goodbying and good lucking, the journey began.

Duffy, who knew the way of course, flew on ahead and the others followed. After they had gone about a fair part of a good distance, they decided to break for a rest and a bit of lunch.

They sat around on some grass and Krowfin, who had the flasks, said, 'I'll be mum,' and poured everyone a nice cup of chickweed tea. Longstint handed out the jangleberry jam sandwiches, and everybody munched and slurped away.

After lunch, the Willigrews continued their journey, passing through large green fields, and deep ponds, which, not surprisingly, were very wet.

As they passed one pond, they were surprised to see a small frog sitting upon a rock at the water's edge. They were even more surprised when it spoke. 'Hello,' it croaked, 'where are you all going?'

Bronglay told the frog about the aliens and their attempt to rescue Morwixx.

'That, my friends, is a noble mission,' remarked the frog. 'We also had one of our number, a fine frog called Ted, turned into a chicken dinner, but, unlike you, we cannot make a long journey to find out what happened to him because we would soon run out of hops.'

'Well,' said Dora, 'if we find Ted, rest assured, we will bring him back to your pond.'

'Would you really,' replied the frog, 'that would be very kind of you; only we miss him very much.'

The little frog croaked once and jumped back into the pond with a loud plop, probably going to tell his friends, and the Willigrews went along their way.

Bronglay and his friends had just started walking away from the pond when Duffy, who landed at their feet and looked a bit flustered, stopped them. 'Strange being up ahead,' he warned, 'I have never seen the like of it before in my whole life.'

'What did you see then, Duffy old chap?' asked Bronglay, looking a bit concerned.

'I can't describe it,' Duffy replied, 'You will have to see for yourselves.'

The Willigrews decided to go and take a peek at this strange thing. Duffy showed them the way and Bronglay told the group to approach with caution. However, caution was on his day off so they had to approach with care, who was working on that day.

Longstint, who was very eager to see this 'thing', led the way, and as they turned a corner in the track between the trees, there it was.

What they saw, struck fear into the hearts of the Willigrews; a large creature with the body of what looked like a red lion, the head of a human man with three sets of fearsome teeth in its mouth.

If that wasn't scary enough on the end of its long tail was a bunch of fierce spikes.

'What on earth is that,' asked Krowfin, not expecting an answer, but getting one from Dora, of all Willigrews.

'I read about this creature once at school,' she said,' it is, I think called a Manticore, and those spikes in its tail are poisonous; it can fire them in any direction. This is one dangerous monster. I thought the Manticore was a myth.'

'Are you sure that it's a myth, it has a man's face, perhaps it's a mythter,' said Krowfin, confused as ever.

After hearing about the poisonous spines, the Willigrews hid behind a bush and peered over at the Manticore, as it looked around for something to eat.

It then lifted its head up and gave out a scream that sounded like a musical instrument, a trumpet or flute or something.

'How weird is that?' asked Dora, 'perhaps it ate an orchestra, and is burping music.'

Bronglay decided to have a vote on whether they would turn back or try to sneak around behind the trees.

Knowing that they had to find Morwixx and Ted, the frog, they voted to do the sneaking bit. Very slowly and quietly, so as not to disturb the creature they crept around behind the bushes.

All was going well until Krowfin slipped and fell through a small bush and out the other side. He tried to sneak back, but too late, the Manticore had spotted him, and, in an instant fired a poisonous dart, which missed him and thudded into a tree just above his head.

Krowfin tried to leg it, but the monster leapt through the air and landed directly in front of him.

Hissing from between its many teeth the Manticore spoke, his words mixed in with the musical sounds again, 'Before you die, my little green snack, I will ask you a riddle, if you do not solve it, I will eat you, but if you do solve it, I will eat you anyway because I feel a bit hungry.'

With its tail, swishing menacingly the monster put its face close to Krowfin's and hissed the words, 'Riddle me this, if it takes a week to walk a fortnight, how many apples in a barrel of grapes?'

Poor Krowfin, as you know, is confused at the best of times, but now he was extremely baffled. The other Willigrews were just going to run out and risk their own lives to try to save their little mate, when, swooping down from the trees came Duffy.

Not thinking of himself, he flew straight between the two and pooed in the monster's eye. Splat, it went, and the Manticore hesitated for a second, turned its attention to the little bird, and shaking its head, gave out a musical scream that sounded like a Philharmonic orchestra.

Duffy was now flying about in circles trying to confuse and distract the Manticore. Then it started firing poisonous spines, wildly, into the air in a rage, but missed Duffy with every shot.

Krowfin had run back behind the bushes to watch the action with the others.

They feared for Duffy's life, but were shocked and amazed to see him fly down and gently land on the back of the Manticore's neck, then start preening his feathers.

'That Duffy is one cool dude,' said an impressed Longstint.

'What is he doing?' gasped Rewsin, 'he will be eaten, for certain!'

The monster was not happy and screaming his loud piping music, he fired a sting directly at Duffy. The Willigrews feared the worst, but just as the sting was about to finish him off, the little bird flew upward.

The venomous sting buried itself deep into the back of the Manticore's head. The little group watched as the monster started to stagger about, squealing and hissing, before losing its balance and crashing onto the ground, poisoned by its own sting, the Manticore was dead.

The Willigrews did not like hurting things, let alone killing them, and as they stood around the Manticore all were feeling relieved but sad. Duffy landed by the monster's head and said, 'Sorry mate, much respect, but you would have done the same to me.'

All, for his bravery and for saving the Willigrews once again, congratulated Duffy.

The little band of adventurers were not feeling so happy now as they resumed their journey. After a while, they decided to stop for a rest and something to eat.

Krowfin poured some tea and handed out the jangleberry dodgy jammers, and they sat quietly eating.

Duffy sat on a branch, gazed at the gloomy group, and tried to think about a way of cheering them up.

'I know,' he chirped, 'let's sing the Willigrew song. I will start, and you can all join in.'

He knew that the little green friends couldn't resist a song, and just as he had expected they did join in.

Down, down where the Willigrews play,
Willying and Grewing all through the day,
Little Rewsin and Great Bronglay,
All down where the Willigrews play.

I love my little warm home,
If I had a choice I'd never roam,
But I must down to the Chickweed Bed,
To keep my chubby family fed.

Down, down where the Willigrews say,
Foam backed carpet and underlay,
Willigrews making pots from clay,
All down where the Willigrews play.

This seemed to do the trick, and half way through the song, everyone was doing the Willigrew dance, hopping around and flicking their earlobes.

Feeling much better now, they carried on with their mission. Duffy flew on to see what was up ahead, hoping it wasn't another mythical creature.

There was nothing out of the ordinary, although he did think, he saw a giant octopus on a stick, but it turned out to be a rotating washing line.

He flew back to the Willigrews to warn them that the aliens were not far up ahead.

'Three left turns, two right turns, a bump in the road and a small stream to cross, and we will be there,' he said.

'Right,' said Bronglay, 'when we get there, let me do the talking, just in case they are a bit dodgy.'

It wasn't long before they approached the gravy boat shaped craft, and all but Bronglay hid behind a bush.

'Here goes,' said Bronglay, not sounding very confident, as he approached the aliens. They were gathered in a slimy group on the grass. When they saw him, one of them pointed and shouted, 'grawm garam blarm!' in alarm.

'Sorry,' explained Bronglay, 'I only speak Willigrew, although I do know a bit of Dranglebinder.'

One of the aliens then moved slurpily across to Bronglay and placed a slimy metal object on his head. Bronglay was a little fearful until he realise that now, when they spoke, he could understand them.

They explained that it was a translatorcodifier.

'What sort of a vegetable are you,' it asked, 'we have never seen one that could walk, before, would it be all right if we ate you?'

'I am not a vegetable,' replied Bronglay looking a bit miffed, 'I am a Willigrew, and

213

under no circumstances do we like being eaten.'

'Well, what are you doing disturbing us at this time of the day if you haven't come to be eaten, we were in the middle of a thinking party?'

'We have come to find out what you did with a young Dranglebinder, and a little frog called Ted. You replaced them with ready meals, which was not a very nice thing to do. May we have them back please?' asked Bronglay, as politely as he could.

'Oh! That,' said the alien, smiling, 'didn't you like the ready meals then, they were from a reputable source, and they contained only pure ingredients and no horsemeat? You see, we mean you no harm, but we are on your planet collecting specimens for the Interesting Creatures of the Universe project on our planet.'

By now, the other Willigrews had come out of hiding and were standing beside Bronglay. Duffy flew down and landed on Dora's shoulder. When the alien noticed the little bird he said, 'Can we take that interesting flappy thing with us as well, that would be very popular with our visitors? We will swap it for a shepherd's pie.'

'Definitely not, you can't just go around taking creatures from their homes and families just as you please, it is very wrong,' said Bronglay, who was starting to lose his patience.

'I tell you what,' the alien continued, 'I'll give you two shepherd's pies, and a chilli con carne and I'll even throw in a tub of sweet and sour sauce for good measure. I can't say fairer than that and I'll take the flappy thing off your hands, wodja say?'

Longstint stepped forward, and a slimy metal thing was placed on his head.

He looked the alien straight in the eye (it only had the one) and said, 'Look, old slimy chap, you don't understand. We do not want ready meals. We want the creatures you kidnapped now. We want to take them back with us, so please tell us where they are, and we will leave you in peace.'

'All right then,' the alien said, 'you drive a hard bargain. I'll chuck in a nice cook-in-the-bag Moussaka, and that's my final offer, take it or leave it. Come on now; be reasonable, all that grub for a little flappy thing.'

By now, Krowfin had stopped listening to the bargaining and had gone over to the spacecraft to have a look around. He was almost sick when he saw what was inside, green and yellow slime covering the walls and floor. He went around the side of the vessel and saw a door, which he tried to open, but he found it locked.

'What I need now,' he thought, 'is someone who can pick a lock, and I know just the very person.'

He beckoned Dora, who crept over behind the aliens.

'I need your GCSE lock-picking skills Dora, can you help?'

'I'll have a go,' said Dora, taking a small pin from under her fur. 'I am not too sure that I will be able to pick an alien lock, I didn't do the alien lock part of the course, so I may have to improvise a bit.'

She tried her normal wiggle, wiggle and waggle method with the pin, but it didn't work. Then she had a thought, she wondered if aliens even knew how to wiggle a pin. She went for the waggle, waggle, waggle and twist method instead. Success, it worked a treat and the door swung open.

Looking, to make sure that the haggling was still going on, Krowfin stepped inside the open door. It was very dark inside so Dora switched on her torch.

What they saw was a bit of a surprise. Not only was Morwixx there and Ted the frog, but there were several other creatures. Among them, there was a rabbit, a newt, two hedgehogs and an extremely large pig with a very curly tail!

Realising that there not much time, Dora told all the creatures to follow her, and be very quiet. All the animals plus Morwixx crept out and followed her over to some bushes, where they hid to await developments.

Krowfin was closing the door, as quietly as he could, when he heard a squeaky little voice. 'Wait for me,' it said, and a little mouse came scurrying out and ran over to Dora in her hiding place.

Meanwhile, back with the haggling, Bronglay was still trying to explain that they thought kidnapping was very wrong and that the aliens should release their captives and return to their planet immediately.

A little way away from the aliens Longstint was now talking to Rewsin. 'I have an idea,' he said, 'what, in your experience, is the thing that sluggy things hate most of all?'

'I haven't a clue,' replied Rewsin, 'is it a badly dressed slug or perhaps a snail with no fashion sense?'

'Good try, 'said Longstint, trying to be kind. 'No, what I am talking about is SALT.'

'Salt,' asked Rewsin, 'you mean the salt you put on your chips?'

'Yes, you see, to slugs salt is very dangerous, it fizzes up their slime and kills them. Don't get me wrong, I am not for one minute suggesting that we harm the aliens in any way, but if they think we have some salt, it might frighten them away.' explained Longstint.

'Wizzo plan,' enthused Rewsin, 'I'm all for that, let's give it a go.'

Longstint proceeded to fill a small paper bag with soil, wrote the word 'salt' on it and walked over to the slimy things.

He greeted them by saying, 'I say you chaps I have a little present for you,' and held the bag up in front of him.

'The aliens became a bit excited and started saying things like, 'ooh! I love presents' and 'is it someone's birthday?'

'What is it?' one of them asked.

'It is a lovely big bag of salt,' shouted

Longstint, waving the bag back and forth.

A look of absolute horror came over the face of the alien that had been bargaining with Bronglay, and he gasped, shakily, 'Did he just say the S word?'

Someone shouted, 'Quick, sound the salt alarm, we are in danger!' and the aliens started to get into the spacecraft.

They were definitely in a panic. Shouting things like, 'keep away from the salt. That paper bag is dangerous, and I want my mum.'

When the alarm sounded, a high-pitched whistling, it had the Willigrews covering their ears.

Everyone watched as the slippery creatures

slithered through the door, unloaded four large crates and climbed slurpily back into the slimy compartment.

As the engines started up a cry went up from Rewsin, 'What about the creatures they kidnapped, shouldn't we help them before the aliens go?'

However, he was relieved when he turned and saw Dora coming back followed by Morwixx and a little trail of forest creatures.

Meanwhile, Krowfin had opened the cases, 'Come and look at this lot,' he shouted.

'These cases are packed with ready meals and jars of cooking sauce. They must have been planning to kidnap a lot more creatures before they went home.'

'Gather round please everyone,' called Bronglay. 'I think I should say a few words. I am sure that everyone will want to thank Longstint and Dora for their quick thinking.'

A round of applause followed this and Longstint blushed a bit.

Krowfin then welcomed the freed prisoners and said that they should all have some food and drink before they started home.

So, sitting around in a circle on the ground, they munched into some chickweed sandwiches. They talked about the day's events and were having a splendid time, until Morwixx squealed, 'Err, gross, this isn't salt its soil.'

She had read the word on the paper bag and, without looking inside had sprinkled her sandwich with the gritty soil.

That set everybody laughing loudly including Morwixx, who also saw the funny side of her mishap.

On the journey back to Willigrew, the kidnapped animals were dropped off near where they lived.

When they reached the pond where Ted lived, however, it looked deserted.

Ted dived under the water and, suddenly, little froggy heads were popping up everywhere.

The pond was full of them, and one said, 'Let's hear it for the Willigrews, are you all ready?'

Then they started to sing a song, which, if I remember rightly, went something like this:

Croak all day, croak all night,
Whether it's dark or whether it's light,
We will croak cos' that's what we do,
We would be happy if you croaked too.

The Willigrews accepted the invitation and joined in with the croaking as sort of backing singers.

We can't read, we can't write,
So we'll keep on croaking if that's all right,
Frogs are green, grass is too,
But I expect you knew that, didn't you.

What followed delighted the audience as the frogs gave a special display of synchronised swimming.

'Brilliant,' said Krowfin, 'and they didn't

even need nose clips.'

After waving good-bye to the frogs, the Willigrews went back home to their village. When they arrived, the Dranglebinders were there.

Duffy had told them about the rescue. At the front of the crowd was Flindax, Morwixx's father. He ran toward his daughter and scooped her up in his arms. Morwixx was delighted to see her dad again, and the happy little family started for their home straight away.

As they walked off, hand in hand, Morwixx said, 'I am very hungry Dad, what's for dinner?' to which Flindax replied, 'To celebrate your homecoming, my darling, I have prepared a delicious Chicken Tikka Masala, especially for you.'

This made all those present laugh aloud, and dance around in a very happy way.

The sparkling mist, unfortunately, had gone now, so they put off the celebrations until the following year.

However, don't worry, I will tell you all about that in another story.

The End

Dear Reader

I hope you have enjoyed these stories

Please visit our website

www.willigrews.co.uk

or follow us on

FACEBOOK or TWITTER

If you have enjoyed the book, would you be kind enough to put a Review on Amazon

Printed in Great Britain
by Amazon.co.uk, Ltd.,
Marston Gate.